The young sow wild oats
The old grow sage

Prologue

_T_he memory of that hot, dry afternoon comes back to me in my dreams.

There we are once again, running to the herb garden. I wrinkle my nose as a pungent, musty odor suddenly invades my nostrils. My first thought is of Thanksgiving dinner, even though it's the middle of July. It's the sage; we're surrounded by it.

That's where we find her, lying, crying in the sage. It's narrow fuzzy leaves lap at our legs as we drop to her side. There's so much confusion around us. Old Winder is barking at the edge of the garden. "Hush Boy," I say. But he doesn't stop. We're unsure of what to do.

The gray-green sage is all around us; sage spotted red with blood. She's screaming at us, but I don't understand what to do. I can't think with her screaming at me and the dog is barking so loud. The baby! Oh no, the baby, she's not breathing! What do we do? The dog won't stop barking. We're covered in blood and we're so afraid.

But then the old woman comes on silent feet. She is withered with hooded eyes- but behind her heavy eyes, shines the wisdom of a thousand scholars. She knows what to do.

The dream always ends the same. "You did good, girls. You did good," she says to us, then smiles. I try to reach for the old woman, but as my fingertips graze her purple woolen skirt, she disappears. The world around us falls silent. And we are happy for the Sage.

Knowledge speaks, but wisdom listens"
Jimi Hendrix

Chapter 1

"Oh No!" Katie Winslow moaned, throwing her hands into the air.

I watched my best friend rummage through her notebook. Her delicate fingers worked nervously through her papers.

"What are you doing?" I said, playfully slapping the back of her head. My desk was behind Katie's, which made it easy to torture my small-framed friend. She hated it.

She laid her head down on the desktop. "I can't find the permission slip."

"What permission slip?" I questioned.

She turned around in her seat, her hand searching her empty shirt pocket. "The permission slip to have me dropped off at Hal's Drive-In.," she said, shaking her head. "If I don't have one, the bus driver will have to drop me off at home- and I'm supposed to meet my parents at the drive-in for a last day of school lunch."

I snickered. "Well, maybe you could write another one." I couldn't help but giggle. If she only knew, I thought. I had seen the note on her desk when she got up to sharpen her pencil, so I took it.

"That would never work." Her eyes narrowed. "Hey, why are you laughing? This isn't funny."

I'm not laughing," I said, covering my mouth with my hand. It was no use, I suddenly burst into an explosion of laughter, which ricocheted off the smooth plaster walls and blasted the ears of everyone in the classroom.

"Sorry," I said softly, and returned an innocent stare to the 25 sets of unblinking eyes that were looking at me.

"Miss Smith, you will stay after class," Ms. Gilmore said, through gritted teeth. Her long crooked nose twitched and she clenched her hands into tight fists.

The bell pealed its last high-pitched call of the year. "Have a good summer Livvy," Katie

said as she snatched her permission slip from my hand. She giggled as she sauntered out of the classroom.

I tapped the bottom of her desk with the toe of my cowboy boot as I waited for the parade of students to pass by me on their way to their buses. They chattered and laughed as they shuffled past. Sarah Mitchell skipped by me saying, Finally Free! Finally free! She was always acting like an idiot.

I folded my arms and slumped down in my desk. This is no fair, I thought. Sweat trickled down the back of my neck under my heavy blonde hair. What a lousy start to my summer break. I wiped the back of my neck as the clamor and laughter of my classmates became distant echoes moving farther down the hall towards freedom.

Finally-silence, and the stomach wrenching realization that I was about to be lectured to. I slumped farther into my seat. Maybe, she won't see me- I tried to fool myself. Maybe she'll be so excited to leave this place that she'll just walk out, forgetting all about me. I'll just hold tight. I won't move a muscle. A smile came over my face.

"Uh, hmm." The sound of Ms. Gilmore clearing her throat shattered my illusion. I bit my lip and squeezed my eyes shut as the tap, tap, tap of high heeled shoes came closer and closer, then stopped.

"Miss Smith, please sit up straight in your desk."

I slowly slid back up, but kept my gaze on my scraped knees. I didn't want to see that familiar expression on Ms. Gilmore's face. I was tired of seeing her tiny eyes peering at me over her crooked nose-her pinched mouth forming those three annoying words, Olivia- I'm-Disappointed.

"Olivia, I'm disappointed."

"I said I was sorry," I mumbled, peering at her through long strands of shaggy hair.

She squeezed herself into Katy's desk, then reached over and lifted my chin. "Olivia, you have so much potential. You're a smart young lady. You're in the top of your class." She paused, smiling at me. "But, you need an attitude adjustment. What is all this clowning around you do? Are you bored in class, or do you feel you aren't getting enough attention at home? You can trust me Olivia." She said, softly.

I squirmed uncomfortably, wiping more sweat off the back of my neck. Summer had kick started early for Washington State. It was only the first week of June and the temperature already hovered just above eighty. "I'm fine, Ms. Gilmore. I guess you can say I'm just a little more active then a lot of your other students. I'm sorry if I'm a pain." I ran a hand over the bumpy scab on my knee. "Can I go now? It's really hot and I don't want to miss my bus." I said, making brief eye contact with her before staring at my knees again.

"Okay, Olivia," she said, standing up. "One piece of advice before you leave. You're almost 13 years old. Why don't you try to look like the young lady you are becoming? Get rid of those cowboy boots, pull your hair away from your face and maybe try on a dress. You might like it and who knows, maybe dressing like a young lady every once in a while might rub off on your attitude." She paused, waiting for my reaction. When she realized she wasn't going to get anywhere with her pep talk, if that's what you wanted to call it, she just sighed and said, "Have a good summer Miss Smith," and pointed to the door.

"The last thing anybody will ever catch me in is a dress," I said, jerking out of my desk and clomping my cowboy boots out the door, down the empty hall and out the large double doors and into the bright sunlight. "Finally Free!" I called out. "Finally free!"

When the bus finally dropped me off in front of the faded picket fence, which surrounded our home, I was soaked. Water dripped off my hair, trickling down my face. I took a lick every once in awhile; I liked the salty taste of sweat and water mixed up.

On the last day of school we are allowed to take squirt guns on the bus. Mr. Homer, our bus driver, always wears a raincoat that day. One year, Jacob Martin filled a squirt gun with milk and squirted everything and everyone in the entire bus with it. Mr. Homer let the bus sit for the entire summer break soaking in the milky mess.

The week before school started he made Jacob clean the inside of the entire bus. Somebody told me the smell was so bad that Jacob threw-up three times. I don't know if that's true or not, but I do know nobody has put anything other than water in their squirt gun since.

"Livvy!" My mom called out, arms opened wide.

"Mom! Did you make pizza like you promised?" I ran to the wide porch of our farmhouse.

She laughed, "Of course, and the root beer floats too." She had a hammer in her hand. Since my dad works as a commercial fisherman, it means that mom and me are left alone *a lot*. We've learned how to do a lot of repairs on our own. My mom's actually a pretty good plumber.

"So, what happened this time," I said, giving her a wet hug.

"Oh, just a couple loose boards. No big deal." She pulled away. "My goodness, you are definitely wet Livvy. Just tell me, no milk this year, right?" She smiled and wiped off the front of her bright pink tank top.

"Nah, I think he learned his lesson."

"Well, my little mermaid why don't you go get out of those wet clothes, and then when you come down, I'll have an extra-special surprise for you in the kitchen," Mom said, pushing me towards the front door.

"Really? What is it?"

She shook her head. Don't even try to get it out of me. You have to wait until you get cleaned up."

"This has turned out to be a pretty good day after all!" I sloshed and clomped all the way up the stairs.

"What do you mean by- turned out to be a good day?" Mom called after me. But I pretended not to hear her.

———

I couldn't find any clean clothes in my room, so I put on my favorite pair of cut-offs (only 3 days on them- should be good for one more) and a white T-shirt I took from my dad's dresser. Ah, comfort, I thought as I padded barefoot back down the stairs. The sounds of clanking dishes in the kitchen climbed the stairs, and quickly, my mind switched gears to my extra special surprise. *Oh please, please*, I hoped. *Let it be Double chocolate cake.* That would taste so good with pizza and root beer floats.

"Okay, Mom! I'm coming down the stairs and I'm ready for my surprise!" The sound of my mom's laughter bubbled up the stairs- pops of tinkling sound rising from the kitchen. I wondered if I had said something funny.

More laughter. I stopped on the bottom step and listened carefully. Was my mom *talking* to herself? Oh great- I mused. She's gone senile.

My imagination started taking over…

She'll have to be put in a home, and since Dad is on a fishing boat half the year, I'm going to be sent to live with Aunt Desta, Uncle Tom and my stuffy cousin Penelope. That would be a nightmare.

I couldn't live with my cousin. She lives under the *delusion* that she's an adult, so she acts too prissy and too mature to do anything fun. Just because her mom was a *model* in New York City, she thought she was so cool.

If you want to know the truth- Penelope is a good old-fashioned spoiled brat- who's too pretty for her own good. I saw her on a magazine cover with her mom once and I wanted to vomit. The article went on and on about how *perfect* they were. Which is definitely *not* true.

The one good thing about having Penelope for a cousin (the only good thing) is that she was born several months before me- saving me from inheriting the horrible family name of *'Penelope'* that has been passed down through the Smith women for about 10 generations.

I always kind have liked Aunt Desta, though. She's Ethiopian, which always made her seem mysterious and exotic to me. A photographer discovered her when she was only 13 while he was in Addis Ababa shooting pictures for some geography magazine. The agency paid for her and her mother to fly to New York and the rest is super model history.

She didn't meet Uncle Tom until years later. He was her lawyer when she sued some tabloid for publishing false information about her. They fell in love, and after she retired, they settled in Seattle, where Uncle Tom and Daddy grew up.

My mom's voice rose again- followed by more laughter.

My life was ruined. I slumped down on the wide fir step and listened as my mom had a conversation with herself.

"Livvy, are you coming? Your surprise is getting tired!"

"On my way! I just had to tie my shoe," I lied. *How could chocolate cake get tired*? I shrugged, and wandered into the kitchen to stand at the side of my senile parent.

The spicy aroma of pepperoni mingled with the cinnamon scented candles Mom had lit in the kitchen. I stood in the doorway and scanned the room for my last day of school treats. I saw my pizza sliced and ready for me on the old butcher block that crowded the middle of our kitchen- my root beer float, in traditional tall plastic bear mug beside it.

I saw a basket of carrots by the sink, which I assumed I would end up cleaning later for dinner. I saw a plate of freshly baked chocolate chip cookies on the counter near the window. I saw...Penelope!

"Tie your shoes? Did someone invent invisible shoes and not tell me. Remind me not to get a pair."

I looked down, remembering my bare feet, then looked back up. She was still there. Yes, there standing in the yellow midday light that poured through our kitchen window was my cousin Penelope.

Her black hair was neatly pulled back into a roll, and her skin, the color of chocolate caramels, was scrubbed and clean. She shone in blue Capri pants and a tight white tee. Her sandals exposed her perfectly painted toenails and stylish toe ring. I couldn't breath. This *was* a nightmare.

"Surprise!" My mom yelled.

I turned to her and silently mouthed "why?"

9

Pushing a piece of pizza into my hand, my mom said, "Penelope is going to spend the summer with us while her parents are in Europe."

I looked at Penelope. She picked up her root beer float and before pursing her perfectly painted lips around her straw, she flashed me a sarcastic smile.

"Oh Boy!" I said, sarcastically waving my arms about my head. "I am so excited! What a perfectly wonderful way to spend my summer break. Gee, Mom," I said, glaring at her. "Thank you for this extra special surprise. What's next Mom? Oh, I know, a fun-filled week touring all of the area slaughter houses." By this time I was out of control. My mom and Penelope just stared at me with their mouths hanging open. I spun around to leave, but accidentally stumbled over my own bare feet, dropping awkwardly onto the wood floor.

"Are you Okay, honey?" My mom whispered, trying to help me up.

"I'm fine," I said, pushing her hand away. I limped, too proud to glance back and see Penelope's expression, silently out the kitchen door.

In the late afternoon a soft breeze always blows across our front porch. It's one of those funny things that you don't pay much attention to, but would miss if it stopped happening- like our creaky step on our staircase, and how the garden gate makes a whiny sound when you open it, and the way the lavender smells when you brush past it in the late summer. Just things- weird things that let you know you're home.

That afternoon, I sat on our front porch step rubbing my sore ankle and letting that soft breeze brush across my face.

"Care for some company?" My mom said, from behind the screen door.

"Sure," I mumbled.

She sat down beside me and grabbed my hand. She was silent for a moment. "How's that ankle?" She finally asked.

"A little sore, but I'll live." I didn't look at her.

"Livvy, I'm sorry. I guess I should have told you we were

going to be taking care of Penelope a long time ago. I just thought it would a fun surprise for you to get to spend summer break with someone your own age. You know, kind of like a summer long slumber party!" She took a breath. "I wasn't thinking, honey. I guess I forgot how little you two have in common."

I didn't answer. I wasn't through being mad at her. We sat there a few more moments together with nothing but the sound of that reliable old breeze tickling the wind chimes. My mom slowly stood up and started to walk back into the house. "Well, I've got a ton of work to do," she said stretching. "Break time is over."

"I already have friends my own age," I finally said. "I don't need another."

My mom sighed. I could tell she was tired of trying to humor me. "Well, Livvy," she said. "It's done and Penelope will be staying here for the next 6 weeks. My advice," she paused. "Get over it! Oh, before you go and hide for the rest of the afternoon I need you take some yarn over to the Wahl's for me. Can you do that?"

"Yeah," I answered numbly. "No problem, as long as Penelope isn't going with me."

Don't worry; she's in the shower. Now get over here and hug me."

I decided to give in and forgive my mom for ruining my summer break. After all, she's only human. And besides, how could she know how much I loathed Penelope. I always told my parents I liked her just fine because she was blood and I didn't want to cause any problems.

What am I suppose to tell my parents anyway, "Uh, hey- Did you know Dad's *only* brother's daughter is snooty and rotten and drives me crazy when I'm around her. I know I only see her twice a year, but could you do me a favor and cause a big rift in the family by letting Uncle Tom know that?" I don't think so.

I gave my mom the biggest bear hug I could manage.

"Oh, whoa girl, so you do love me!" My mom said, squeezing me with equal force.

"Yeah, I'll forgive you this time," I said breaking away. "But if you mess up again, Ill have to let you go."

She laughed. "Oh, is her highness threatening her overworked, under appreciated, under paid maid?"

I fought back a giggle and tried to look pompous. "Yes."

She laughed again and messed my hair. "Go- the bag of yarn is on my craft table."

I waved as I took off across the porch. I heard my mom yelling behind me,

"Be back within 45 minutes or I send out the posse." But, I pretended not to hear.

"Don't judge each day by the harvest you reap but by the seeds that you plant."
Robert Louis Stevenson

Chapter 2

We live on Apple Road. It's a "U" shaped road that's about five miles long and connects to Highway 20 at both ends. A long time ago, Apple Road was where several large orchards were. Our farm was one of them. My Great - Great Grandpa Finn built the farmhouse and barns from timber harvested from our property. He planted ten varieties of apple trees, two varieties of plum tree, raspberries, and two varieties of grapes.

After my great-great grandparents died, the farm was passed down to my great grandpa, then my grandma, and finally my mom.

None of the old orchards around here are still operating. The old Paige farm was turned into a Bed and Breakfast by a rich Seattle couple. They call it "Orchard Mill," which is dumb. I don't remember a mill anywhere on the property. When old Mrs. Whitmore died a few years ago, her farm was divided between her 5 grown-up children. They chopped it up into 10-acre tracts. Every time one sells, we see another mobile home where there were once beautiful old fruit trees. As for our farm, only the ghosts of a more affluent time remain; rusty old apple pickers hung on the barn walls under a veil of cob webbing, the occasional old crate with the Finn logo, the bones of an apple press slowly disintegrating.

I clutched mom's overfilled paper bag. Skeins of yarn in all colors were pouring out the top. I kept shoving them back in, but every time I did, more would fall out.

I usually complained when Mom asked me to run an errand for her, but never if she asked me to go to the Wahl's. You see- they have a son named Jared. He never paid much attention to me. He just turned 14 and he thought I was goofy. I wasn't trying to act goofy. It was just that whenever I was around him, something happened to my brain. I don't know why, but part of it stopped working and I always ended up saying something stupid.

"Ouch!" I yelled, dropping the bag of yarn and spilling its contents all over the road. I hopped up and down rubbing my sore ankle. "Man," I grunted. "I did it again!"

"Howdy, Maam. That looks like a mighty hurt leg."

"What?" I turned on my good foot to find the Wahl twins, Caleb and Elijah. Two 5-year-old redheaded oddballs were what they were!

"I say," Caleb said, tipping his battered black cowboy hat, "You look like you got a mighty hurt foot."

"Oh, yeah, I just tripped a couple of times that's all." I bent down and started picking up tangled balls of yarn. "You boys want to help me here. As you can see, there's yarn everywhere." I forced a kind smile.

"Oh, no thanks," Caleb said, rubbing his stubby nose. "Cowboys don't pick up yarn and we gotta go get us some gad guys- I mean bag guys- I mean."

"Bad guys," Elijah said, then growled.

"Oh, thanks buddy. I was a bit confused for a minute there." Caleb patted his brother on the head. "He's a dinosaur today."

"Oh, I said, trying not to bust out laughing. I see."

"Well, we have to go now." Caleb turned; his spurs clinked as he moseyed down the road.

"Come on dinosaur buddy," he called not looking back. "We got bad guys to catch."

Elijah growled a farewell then scurried off to catch up with his brother.

I finished picking up the yarn; stuffing it as best I could back into the now ripped paper bag.

When I finished I looked up to find Jared watching me from his driveway.

I limped as elegantly as I could muster past him.

"Hi Jared," I squeaked.

"Hey Livvy," he said, staring past me. "Did you happen to see the twins?"

"Yeah, I just talked to the little oddballs." I suddenly felt very warm. I couldn't believe I just called his little brothers oddballs right in front of him.

"Excuse me?" he said.

" I mean- they were just helping me pick up these odd balls of yarn I dropped on the road." I smiled, thinking I had just pulled off the best save ever.

He just stared at me blankly for what seemed like an eternity, then finally said, "Well, okay then, Livvy, I guess I'll see you later."

"Okay, Jared, I'll see you later," I responded, smiling way too wide.

He turned and gave me one of those looks. You know- the look you give someone with a booger hanging from his or her nose.

I watched him jog down the gravel drive until he disappeared into the trees, leaving only a low brown rising of dust where he had once stepped. I was truly pathetic.

The Wahl's old shingled farmhouse had never seen a coat of paint or varnish in its one hundred years. The once red brown cedar shingles still fragrant from pitch, over time, had turned soft silver gray. With the afternoon sun, they reminded me of moth wings shimmering soft silver under a porch light at night.

Over their porch rail hung a beautiful wedding ring quilt. It was made in patchworks of reds, blues and yellows. It blended beautifully with the flower boxes that overflowed with red petunias, blue lobelia and yellow snapdragons.

Jared's mom and dad were nice. They tended to be what I call of the granola variety - extra crunchy. What I mean to say is that they live very naturally. They raise their own animals, using the wool from the sheep to spin into yarn, the milk from the cows they drink and use to churn butter. They grow their own fruits and vegetables in a huge garden and every season you'll find them scouring the woods for mushrooms or roots or weeds to eat or concoct some medicinal tea out of. I have a hard time understanding it. They seem to work way too hard for things that could be easily picked up ready made at the local grocery store.

Mrs. Wahl came from behind the house. She wore her hair in braids that hung like two gold ropes down her back. I had never seen her in any other hairstyle. I noticed she didn't even need rubber bands to hold the braids together. But the braids were never messy, always smooth and shiny. Their old golden retriever, Winder, followed close on Diane's heels. He stopped and started to bark, but not at me. He was pointed toward the field barking at the grass that seemed to whisper as it swayed with the breeze.

You see- Winder never barks at real people, only spirits. At least that's what the Wahl's believe.

"Winder," Mrs. Wahl reprimanded. "Go bark at some other poor soul. You're disrupting our visitor. Winder tucked his tail between his legs and crawled, defeated, behind the house. "Livvy, what brings you this way," she said, rubbing her very pregnant belly. The sun was behind her showing her curves through the white sundress she was wearing. How could a woman's stomach stretch to that size without exploding, I wondered.

"My mom gave me this bag of yarn to bring to you." I held out my crinkled brown-bagged offering. A skein of deep purple yarn fell to the ground. I scurried to pick it up, but dropped the rest of the yarn in the process. "I'm sorry, I said. "I can't seem to keep this stuff in the bag today."

"Sometimes yarn does take on a life of its own," she said, smiling. "Let me help you." She squatted down and started gathering up the now unraveling skeins.

"Mrs. Wahl, should you be doing that?" I grabbed her arm to steady her.

"Livvy," she said, pulling me free. "I weeded a half acre garden today and milked a cow without any problems at all. I think I can pick up a few stray balls of yarn. And please, Livvy," she continued. "Don't call me Mrs. Wahl. It makes me feel like a very old woman."

"I keep forgetting." I said and handed her the desperately battered bag. "I'm so used to calling all the adults at school Mrs. Something or Mr. Something, that I just say it to all adults now."

"Well, I'm still trying to talk your mom into home schooling," she said, standing up. She clutched the full bag of yarn as if it would come alive and jump from her arms. "Home schooling has done our family a lot of good. Made us a closer family."

"Great," I said, thinking there was no way I was falling for that. As much as I hate having to get an education, I think I would hate it more being given to me by my mom.

"How does a nice tall glass of Iced Tea sound?" She asked, smiling so sweetly, she almost seemed kind of young for a moment. Mom always said Diane Wahl was young for having a 14 year old. But I think everybody seems young to someone who is 38. Ancient.

"Oh, I can't. Mom said she would send the posse after me if I didn't get right home."

"Another time."

"Yeah, well, I'll see you later Mrs.- I mean Diane."

"Tell your mom thank you for me," she said, slightly raising the mangled brown bag.

As I strolled down the dusty drive, I saw Jared and the twins walking through a tall grassy field.

The afternoon sun lay as a golden blanket across the field. He was knocking a path through the grass, while the twins stumbled behind. Elijah was still growling and snarling. Both boys were oblivious to what a nice a brother he was to them. I wish Jared liked me as much.

I walked back to my house slowly. I imagined arriving home and mom saying, "Oh honey, I'm sorry, Penelope is gone. Her parents decided not to go to Europe! They picked her up. You just missed her." But deep inside I knew I wasn't that lucky. I took a deep breath as I climbed our porch steps.

This was going to be the worst summer of my life!

"Angry people are not always wise."
Jane Austen,

Chapter 3

"Hey Livvy," my mom called from the kitchen. "Did you get the bag to her in one piece?"

"Well, let me put it this way," I said, closing the front door. "She got the yarn."

Mom poked her head through the kitchen door. "What do you mean by she *got* the yarn? Please, don't say *got*. You sound like a hick."

"Mom, I am a hick. What's for dinner?" I said, stumbling up behind her. "It smells fishy in here."

"It's tuna casserole." Mom popped me on the head with a carrot she was peeling.

"Oh, Mom, do you actually think Princess Smarty-Pants is going to eat something like tuna casserole?"

Mom rolled her eyes. "Yes, of course she will. You might be surprised, I'll bet they have casseroles every once in awhile." She smiled, then added. "Though, they're probably eating caviar or lobster casseroles." We both snickered, and then mom hushed me when we heard the stair squeak.

Now, I love my home. I love everything about it. I love its sounds; it's squeaks and hums. I love the way the kitchen smells after

18

a pancake breakfast. I love the way the barca lounger feels after my dads been in it - the leather is soft and warm and smells of Old Spice. But hearing the stair squeak, the very sound that usually warms my heart, under the foot of Penelope made my skin crawl.

"Hey," she said, poking her perfect face around the kitchen door.

"Hey, Penelope," Mom said. "Did you enjoy your shower?" Mom handed me a paring knife and motioned me to the sink to finish cleaning the carrots. "Come on in and join us Penny. There's some broccoli that needs to be cut up." Mom wiped a stray chestnut strand away from her face with the back of her wrist.

I love my mom's hair. It's thick and lays in dark waves down her back. In the sun her dark trusses have a copper glow. For being pretty old, I think my mom is actually kind of pretty. I wish she wore it long more often, but she doesn't. She usually wears it in a French roll. Except when Dads home, that's the only time she wears it long.

I, unfortunately, have inherited my father's coarse blonde hair. It so wants to be curly, but can't make up its mind. So- my hair just hangs there, kind of like a frizzy horses' tail. My mom says she thinks my hair is beautiful. But, she would have to say I was beautiful even if I had corncobs growing from my eyes.

"You want me to cut the broccoli?" Penelope asked. She came into the kitchen wearing a blue and yellow plaid sundress. I wouldn't wear a dress to dinner if we were being served lobster and eating with the queen, let alone tuna casserole with my cousin.

"I think you can handle it." Mom pushed a head of broccoli into her hands and motioned her to stand by me. "I'll be right back, girls. I'm going to the green house to fetch some nice ripe tomatoes."

"You have cut broccoli before, haven't you?" I questioned.

She curled her lip at me.

"Oh, come on Penny, that's not a face." I crossed my eyes and stuck my tongue out, touching it to the tip of my nose. I was very proud of that face. I still am the only one in my class who can do it.

"That's disgusting." She looked away.

" I bet you can't do it." I made the face again.

She slammed the broccoli down onto the granite counter top. It landed with a squashy thud. "Who would want to," she barked.

"Look here, *Livvy*," she spat my name out like it was vinegar on her tongue. "I'm only here because I have to be. I'm only going to speak to you when I have to, so don't try to impress me with your hillbilly humor. I don't care for anything about you or your stupid backwoods ways. Do I make myself clear, *Livvy*?"

She glared at me. There was real anger behind that stare, and for the first time in my life I was speechless. "By the way, my name is Penelope," she continued. "Don't ever call me Penny. I'm only allowing your mother to call me that because I don't want her to hate me and make me more miserable than I already am."

"Fine." I grunted. We chopped and peeled in silence for what felt like an eternity, until finally, I heard my mom's familiar footsteps coming towards the house.

"Okay, here we go," Mom came in muttering to herself. "Some nice homegrown tomatoes." She placed the tomatoes on the counter near where Penelope was cutting broccoli. "Whoa! Penny, what did that broccoli do to you?"

"What do you mean Aunt Claire?" Penelope turned and looked doe-eyed at my mother.

Talk about Dr. Jekyll and little Miss Hyde, I thought.

My mom was trying her best to keep a straight face. "Oh nothing, honey. It's just that, well," she paused. "It's okay, we can use a spoon."

I peeked over to Penelope's cutting area. Scattered across the countertop, like spilled ice cream sprinkles, lay hundreds of tiny florets that she had cut completely off the broccoli stalks. "Nice job, *Penny*! I smirked. "We can just sprinkle those over the casserole."

"Livvy, be nice." My mom warned.

Penelope turned and glared at me again. This time, I swear her eyes practically shot nails at me.

"What is for dinner, Aunt Clair?" Penelope asked Mom, sweetly.

"Oh, it's tuna casserole." Mom said, opening the refrigerator and looking for the salad dressing. And as usual, she quickly added. "Home canned tuna, of course."

I don't know why but my mom thinks its automatically better if its either, home canned, homegrown or homemade.

I always try to tell her that it's not always the case. Let me use my mom's friend Regina Frostman for an example- which is fitting because she looks like a snowman. Really! Her entire body looks like a stack of perfect spheres. She has a big round head, attached to an even bigger round torso, attached to a frightfully large round bottom- just like a snowman. Anyway, she puts away cucumbers every year, and they taste like she pickles them in gasoline. I hate them. I don't think I know one person who would prefer her pickles to store bought. Whenever anybody hears Regina say, "It's home canned," they cringe. But every year she brings over quarts of them, and my parents make me eat one in front of her just to be nice.

"Oh, wow!" Penelope said. "What a treat. I don't think I've ever eaten home-canned tuna before."

I saw my mom smile to herself. Then she switched gears, saying, "Why don't you girls grab the utensils and set up the picnic table while I finish up in here."

We both reluctantly agreed.

Dinner went pretty quietly. Penelope politely commented on Mom's casserole several times. Mom nervously chattered about all the fun things we could together, all the while, scattering broccoli sprinkles across our salads. As for me, my mind drifted. Tomorrow was payback. What would it be, water balloons, or perhaps cow patty bombs?
Nah, I knew it had to be more creative than that. I decided to sleep on it.

That night I cozied up under crisp white sheets as the weak light of a crescent moon played softly across the folds of my tattered quilt. Lucky for me, we have a spare bedroom, so my room was still my own.

The wallpaper is a really old pattern of big cottage roses that, over time, have faded to soft tea stained shades of pink and green. My mom says it needs a good paint job, but she just can't bring herself to rip it down. My great-grandmother hung the paper for my grandmother when she was little. This was my mom's room too.

Mom says generations of laughter and song are locked within this room. I think she's right. Sometimes if I'm very quiet and listen very hard, I swear I can her Great-Grandma singing that old lullaby Mama said she used to sing to Grandma. *"Hush-a-bye, don't you cry, go to sleep my little baby. When you wake, you will find, all the pretty little horses."*

This room is special, and there was no way I was going to let Penelope intrude. Besides, she might interfere with my rooms balance. My room moves around my three piles of clothes: the dirty pile, the not so dirty pile, and the pretty darn clean pile. My friend, Katie, says it's very feng shui. Yeah, sleep came easy that night, for the next day, I would have my revenge.

"Honesty is the first chapter in the book of wisdom."
Thomas Jefferson

Chapter 4

My bed is against a large French paned window on the east side of my room. Ever since I was little, I've liked to wake with the sun warming my face.

That morning was no different. I woke slowly, as I always do, absorbing as much sunlight as I possibly could. Dad says I must be half lizard. In that land that I love, somewhere between sleep and wake, my mind works best. Since I had had no dreams that I could remember, I let the morning rays work on my mind. And that morning my mind tumbled and churned! It was perfect and fail-proof. I would have her crying to go back to the city before lunch!

The corners of my mouth turned up. It was going to be a good day!

By the time Penelope had showered and fixed her hair, tried on about 10 different outfits and painted her toes to match the outfit she had finally picked out, I was done with breakfast and standing beneath the arms of a giant Big Leaf Maple in the field behind the barn. Chickens clucked happily and Daisy, our duck, waddled around in her usual circles.

A few years ago, my Dad hung a tire swing for me off one of the tree's thick high branches. It took him a long time because our ladder was too short to reach the branch. So, there he stood, balanced on the top rung of the ladder with my mom holding the bottom yelling, "You're going to kill yourself! Is it worth your life?!"
Well, finally, after a few near slips, my dad did it. He got my swing hung from a heavy moss jacketed branch twenty feet up the tree. He was so proud. We played on it all evening. I remember the exhilaration of the wind in my face. I felt free. I fell in love with the starts that night- and I've been trying to pluck them out of the sky ever since.

Boy, I'm sure going to miss that old tire swing, I thought as I flipped out the blade of my pocket knife.

My parents would kill me if they knew what I was about to do. I took a deep breath and moved my hair away from my eyes. I felt something creamy gush between my left foot toes. "Chicken poop. Yuck!" I said, trying to rub it off in the grass. There was still a fair amount of the white sticky poop stuck between my toes when I climbed onto the old bald truck tire that was tied to that big old tree. I climbed-to the top of the tire, grasping my soiled toes around the knotted off rope.

I took the pocketknife out again. I had to cut the rope so it would hold her until I got it going good and high, then, CRASH! She would hit the ground. I couldn't wait to see her balled up and sobbing in the chicken poop!

With every cut of the knife, the swing moved slightly, which made it hard to keep my balance. My hair tumbled back into my face and sweat trickled down my arm. This was turning out to be harder than I thought.

The barn door squeaked. Barely able to see through all the hair hanging in my face, I stopped to listen, Daisy quaked and slapped her webbed feet against the cement entry of the barn.

I sighed. "Just the duck." I said, and started to cut again.

"Don't you mean just Jared and the duck," I heard Jared's voice behind me.

My heart started pounding in my throat. And in a desperate attempt to conceal my crime, I threw my pocketknife and promptly fell to the ground-landing square on my bottom. I lifted my hair out of eyes. Yep, there he stood. His blonde hair blew loosely around his face. His soft rounded features ethereal in the mornings gentle rays. "Oh, Hi Jared. You startled me," I squeaked.

"I was dropping off a bouquet my mom put together for your mom. Your mom sent me out here to find out what you were up to. So," he cleared his throat. "What are you doing out here?"

"Oh, I said. "I was just playing on my swing."

"Pretty weird way to swing. But I guess you have always done things a little," he paused searching for the kindest word he could come up with. "Well, different." He turned to leave. "By the way, what ever you threw in the grass." He turned back and smiled at me. " You're never going to find it."

"Thanks, Jared." I said, stupidly sitting in what I was positive was more chicken poop.

"Oh, he said, before disappearing behind the barn, "I met your cousin." His eyes sparkled. "She's nice!"

I did not like the way this was beginning to look!

I searched for something to say about her- something that would put a stop to his obvious blossoming insanity. "She's from the city!" I yelled, as he disappeared around the corner.

"I know!" His voice echoed from the other side of the barn.

I just sat there in the grass with chicken poop between my toes and under my seat, until I knew he was out of earshot before... "NOOOO!" Yes, I screamed! I screamed at the top of my lungs! I screamed so loud, I quieted the chickens and stopped Daisy duck in her tracks. My insanity didn't end there. I decided to punish the grass too. I pulled up clods of grass and threw them as hard as I could. Dust rose into a cloud, polluting my eyes and nose, which caused me to sneeze. I wiped my face with my filth-covered hand.

The thought of Jared with that stupid googly-eyed expression on his face made me want to slap him. Jared had become a traitor.

"What are you doing?" Penelope stood poised in red gingham short-alls and denim blue t-shirt with a red bandana tied around her slicked back hair.

"Oh, that would be none of your business." I said, pretending not to be startled by her sudden presence. I stood. "Looks to me by *somebody's* outfit that *somebody's* trying to fit in with her new country surroundings." I said, smugly.

She folded her arms. "To fit in with these surroundings I would have to roll around in a pig pen about 50 times, and I'm not willing to go that far."

I felt like punching her just then. But, I managed to force a smile. "Would you like to try out my tire swing Penelope?"

"What?"

"Come on," I ran over to her and grabbed her arm. "It'll be fun! It will feel just like flying! I promise!"

Penelope pushed me away like I had the plague. "Get away from me, Hillbilly!" she barked. "Why would I want to swing on that thing?"

"I'm sorry if I offended you. I'm just trying to be a good hostess." I rubbed my shoulder. For a city girl, she had a lot of strength.

"Yeah, I'm so sure." She turned back towards the house. "Besides, you probably cut the rope," she mumbled as she stomped away.

I couldn't believe she had just said that! She didn't trust me. Okay, so it was true, I had cut the rope. But for her to accuse me of it, how dare she!

"Okay, fine- so you don't like to swing." I said, scrambling to catch up with her. The aroma of chicken poop clung to the air surrounding me. I was starting to attract flies. "How about horseback riding? I'll take you this afternoon." I caught up with her. "You can ride Pumpkin. She's very gentle."

"Get away from me!" She crinkled her nose and gave me another hard push. "Geez, you stink! She continued towards the house wiping her hands off on her short-alls. "I don't have time for your games," She called back. " Besides, I'm going for a walk with your neighbor, Jared, this afternoon."

The earth stopped spinning at that moment. Penelope Smith might as well have thrown a rock and hit me square in the head. I was numb. I tried to think of something I could say to stop her. But the only thing that came out of my mouth was, "They eat weeds!"

She turned briefly to glower at me with her dark eyes, and then

26

continued into the house.

The air stopped moving and a lump formed in my throat. I felt as if I couldn't breath. I slumped into the grass on the edge of the garden and closed my eyes.

What had happened to my wonderful day? Plan Revenge had backfired. The only boy in the whole area who didn't think sucking spaghetti through one's nostrils should be included as an Olympic event had turned against me. And to top everything off, I was covered in chicken poop and attracting every fly east of Seattle. You could have said my day literally stunk! And I wasn't sure, but I thought I could faintly hear the sound of bells.

SMACK!

"Ouch!" I yelled. It felt like a tractor had just driven into my shoulder. I opened my eyes. My mom was towering over me like a Christmas tree. She was dressed in green over-alls and dangling with garden tools.

"Sorry, Honey." Mom patted my sore shoulder. "I was trying to swat a horse fly that was about to have you for lunch."

"Is that Dad's tool belt?" I said, noticing the gray leather belt that I used to know to hold a hammer and nails now holding twist ties and garden shears.

"Yeah, I cut it down to fit my waist and reconstructed some of the loops and pockets to hold gardening supplies." Mom spun on her boots like a fashion model. "So, what do you think?"

"I think Dad's going to kill you." I said, awkwardly getting back up on my feet.

"This is an old one, your dad's not going to care."

"No, That's his good one."

"Livvy," Mom's voice turned smug. "Your father uses the brown one. You know, the one with the extra loops."

"Mom, don't you remember, he decided he didn't like the brown one because it didn't have that double pocket thingy. So, he bought the gray one." I pointed to her belt.

"Oh," Mom's eyes narrowed. "You know, I think you're right." She shrugged. "Oh well, I guess you better remind me to stop by the hardware store before he gets back." She laughed as she strode into the garden- jingling all the way.

"Hey Livvy," she added, as she disappeared around the corn. Why don't you take Penny horseback riding this afternoon? But don't let her ride Pumpkin; you know how she bucks. And Livvy, I don't know what you were doing this morning," she added. "But you smell like you've been rolling in the chicken coop. Take a shower."

I opened my mouth, but no words escaped. I didn't have the strength.

As I walked into the house, I noticed the front screen door had been left open. Penelope must have forgotten to close it. Good. That's one of Mom's pet peeves. At least I'll have something to bring up at dinner, I thought.

I had started up the stairs, when I thought I heard someone talking in the kitchen. Not happy gossipy chatter either. It was that low whispery menacing kind of talk. You know, the kind of talking you do when you don't want someone to know you're saying mean things about him or her in their own home. I crept towards the kitchen and crouching low at the door, listened to Penelope quietly complain to someone at the other end of our telephone.

"I don't think I can take this much longer," she whispered. "I can't talk louder, you never know when *she'll* show up. My cousin is a cold sore-a blemish on society."

Immediately an urge to march into the kitchen and throttle Penelope began to rise from my stomach. I knew that wouldn't be smart, so I took one of those deep cleansing breaths that Mom's instructor on her yoga video is so into.

I just don't fit in here," she sobbed. "I don't feel like I'm one of them. I think Aunt Claire is trying, but she's uncomfortable with me too." She was quiet for a moment. "Why? Why do you think? Do I have to spell it out for you? I am the only black person in the whole county."

What was she saying? The arrogant little miss fashion model, queen of the penthouse, ballerina extraordinaire, felt she didn't fit in with *us*? And what was this- *do I have to spell it out for you*, nonsense? Does she actually think we care what color her skin is? *Me, me, me-* is that all she ever thought about? What a spoiled brat. She ended the conversation in Spanish. "Adios, Maria. Me hace falta."

Oh, she thinks she's so sophisticated. I would show her a thing or two. I cleared my throat to announce my arrival and swung open the kitchen door, almost hitting her with it.

"Watch it!" She snapped.

"Sorry, I didn't know you were in here. Next time, I'll knock before entering my *own* kitchen."

"Whatever."

"Well, I've got to go and get changed for our walk." I lied. "I'll see you later."

"Excuse me!" She seemed surprised.

"Jared invited me too." It was all I could do to keep eye contact. I felt I was failing as a liar.

"Great." She said, storming past me. "If anyone needs me I'll be in my room drowning my sorrows with Bronte."

I chuckled. I couldn't believe she bought it. My giddiness quickly turned sour, as I came to the realization that if I had to lie to Penelope, I would also have to lie to Jared. How would I manage that? I would consider my twisted tale as I got ready. I bound up the stairs-deception on my mind.

"When people will not weed their own minds, they are apt to be overrun by nettles.
" Horace Walpole

Chapter 5

*J*ared came to the door. He didn't see me peeking at him through the window. He was wearing a freshly tie-died purple and red tee shirt and hole free 501 jeans. He knocked again, and then glanced into the window to catch a glimpse of his reflection. He was checking himself out in the same window that I was peeking through. He didn't see our faces come together, but ran his hand through his long wispy bangs and checked his teeth for food.

He knocked a third time. This time I answered the door. "Hey Jared!" I tried to sound breathless. "I was upstairs, reading Shakespeare. I hope you didn't stand out here too long."

"Not too long," he said, then smiled. "Is Penelope ready?"

I tried to look concerned. "Oh, she's in the bathroom, again."

"I hope she's not sick." He crinkled his nose.

"Oh, she'll be fine. I guess she's not used to good old fashioned country cookin'." Then I whispered, "gives her gas."

He raised his eyebrows. "I see."

I smiled. He smiled. A nervous silence settled into the room. I had to do something, it felt too weird to just be standing there staring at each other. I cleared my throat, rattling the still air. "Well, I guess

I should call her down so we can get going on our walk."

"We?" He questioned.

"Oh, didn't I tell you," "She was a bit nervous about going, so she asked me to come along."

"Oh," he said, looking dazed. "Okay, that will be just fine." He scratched his head.

"Oh Jared," I put my hand on his shoulder. "I feel like I'm intruding. If you want, I can tell her I'm not feeling well. I'm sure since you're already here, she would go without me."

"No, Livvy, it's okay. It's just a walk." He smiled. Yeah, it'll be fine."

Good answer, Jared, I thought. He had just saved himself from an old fashioned punch in the stomach.

"PENELOPE!" I hollered. "JARED'S HERE!" I turned back toward Jared and smiled.

He was grimacing. I guess I was too loud. I wondered, gazing at his contorted features of his scowl, if he had noticed my braided hair. I twisted the thick rope around my fingers.

"Do you think she heard you?" He asked. "Maybe you should go up." He motioned towards our massive fir staircase.

"No need," rolled sweetly from the top of the stairs. It was Penelope. "I think all of Skagit County could hear her." Penelope's steps were so graceful, she seemed to float down the staircase.

I watched Jared watch her. His cheeks flushed and his lips twisted into a sheepish, half- witted grin.

I had to break the spell. "Well, let's get going before it gets too hot." I said, pushing Jared out through the front door. My long heavy braid swung around and smacked him in the face as we lurched into the afternoon light.

Penelope had changed her clothes, yet again. This time she was wearing a pair of fringed denim shorts and a very bright white peasant top. Her leather sandals must have been fresh out of the box. I didn't notice even one scuffmark on them. I couldn't help but wonder how many clothes she had brought, and how that poor old wooden closet rod was managing the weight of them all?

"Well, Livvy, you combed your hair. What a treat." She grabbed Jared's arm and pushed past me.

"Your braid looks nice, Livvy." Jared said and winked at me, as they strolled ahead onto the road.

My heart leapt. I couldn't move. Was I hearing things? Because I had thought Jared, who never pays attention to me, had just paid me a compliment. I was ecstatic. Right there, standing beside Mom's prized pink divinity hybrid tea rose, I vowed to never take that braid out again.

"Are you coming, or are you just going to stand there with that stupid look on your face all day?" Penelope barked.

I stumbled clumsily to catch up. My feet were sweating, and noisily started to slip inside my boots. "I guess I shouldn't have worn these boots," I felt the need to explain the noise. "They're making my feet squeak."

"Feet squeaking? Yeah, right." Penelope smirked. "I'm not so sure it's your feet- sounds more like flatulence."

I knew exactly what that word meant. I felt my face heat up. I usually don't get embarrassed easily, but like I said before, when I was around Jared, I was not the same.

We walked together for a long time. Okay- they walked together for a long time; I was just the squeaky third wheel, stumbling behind them.

We walked along Apple road- my road- the road I grew up along, and was so familiar with, I could be blindfolded and find my way down it by sound alone. The first half-mile is punctuated by the sound of hundreds of croaking frogs that call the large pond over at "Orchard Mill" home.

Once we get to the Wahl's, the frogs are just a hushed murmur and the music changes to that of the human kind. Most days you can hear the soft sounds of a jazz station Diane likes to listen to while she's out in the garden. If she's not listening to music, she's making it. She sits on the porch, strumming a classical guitar, while the twins doodle or play with toys around her feet. She always stops to wave if she sees me, or sometimes she will bring me an apple or a cookie.

As the three of us strolled past Jared's home, it was the radio that was playing. The silky sound of a jazz saxophone rode softly through the air. In the distance, we could see Jared's mom and the twins weeding the vegetable garden, but she didn't hear Jared when he called out.

Penelope didn't seem too impressed. Anyway, she was too busy bragging about the penthouse apartment they own in Seattle and their condo in Hawaii. She blabbed on about private school and piano and dance lessons. She talked on and on about designer clothes and trips abroad. Jared couldn't get a word in to save his life. At one point, I watched him try to point out a beautiful doe and her faun that were nibbling on shrubs just off the road. Penelope was too busy yakking about her favorite Thai restaurant to see them, so Jared looked back to me and motioned towards them. I smiled then mouthed, "Nice."

We walked another mile. Stellar Jays squawked and shook the spidery limbs of the vine maples they were perched on- until the hum of old man Massingale's generator started up and rattled the air, quieting the Jays.

We were approaching Willow creek, one of my favorite places. One of the last of the old wooden plank bridges crosses it to this day. The planks are set far enough a part to drop rocks between to the creek, which rushes 30 feet below. I was never allowed to walk this far away from home when I was little, but sometimes, I would do it anyway.

One time, when I was six, my parents had bought me a new pair of running shoes. The shoes were paper white with small pink flowers embroidered on the sides of them. To test them out, I decided to walk to the bridge.

As soon as I stepped onto the old bridge, I tripped and my left foot became stuck between two of the planks. I struggled to get my foot free, but the only way it was coming out was if I loosened my shoe. Oh so carefully, I untied the crisp white lace. Oh so gingerly, I pulled my bare foot out of the shoe. Oh so cautiously, I tried to dislodge the empty shoe from between the boards, but my little fingers weren't quick enough, and I watched in horror as my new paper white running shoe, with pink flowers embroidered on the side, splashed into the frothy folds of the waters below.

Desperately, I clambered down the weedy, briar entangled bank to the creek's edge and tried to retrieve my shoe. I found it 20 feet down stream, pinned by rushing water against a large moss covered boulder in the middle of the creek.

Now maybe it was because I was six, or maybe it was because I was desperate, but I had made the decision to wade into the creek and get my shoe. I took off my remaining shoe, and plunged my feet into the icy water. The knee-deep water slapping against my legs, felt like a million shards of glass hitting me over and over.

I wanted to get out, but I couldn't move- I had suddenly realized the power of the water, one step and I would be swept down stream. My legs were beginning to become numb and my skin was purple with the cold. I had to get out. Instead of trying to turn around, I decided to take a step backwards. The water would be less swift and if I did fall, I was hoping I could grasp one of small willow trees that grew along the creeks edge, and pull myself to shore.

I held my breath. My feet had begun to ache with the cold, but slowly, I was able to lift my left foot and place it one step back. Now, I thought, if I could do the same with the right foot, I'd be okay. Slowly, I tried to do the same maneuver, but before I had transferred any weight at all, I slipped, plunging into the current.

Hitting the water was like hitting cement, and before I knew it, I had been slammed against a large pointed boulder near the edge of the creek several feet from where I was pulled under. Cold and fear had set in; I couldn't move. I remember opening my mouth to call for help, but I don't remember making any sound. I thought I saw a figure in the woods. Was it Mama? I wondered. I wanted to go to sleep. Everything became dark.

The next thing I remember was waking up on the side of the creek with an old wool sweater wrapped around me. I felt dazed and sore, but the sun was high and had started to warm me. That was the first time I saw the old woman- I knew of her from stories I had been told at school. Her name was Stella and I knew she was a witch. She was busy picking morel mushrooms from underneath a Cottonwood tree and humming some strange tune. Frightened, I tore off the sweater and scurried up the bank and back towards home as fast as my tired, battered legs would let me.

When I got home, I collapsed into my mother's arms and confessed the whole horrid event. Besides, being grounded to my room for a week, Mom visited Stella's cottage and thanked her for saving my life with fresh cut flowers and an apple pie. My shoes were never seen again.

"The simple things are also the most extraordinary things, and only the wise
can see them."
Paulo Coelho

Chapter 6

Though I had had that one bad encounter with the creek, I
never let it frighten me away. Don't get me wrong, I'm not totally
stupid, I have grown to respect its power. I have never since put even
one toe in it. But strangely, I am comforted when I walk over this
bridge. There's something about the sound of water rushing over stone
that soothes me.

Penelope was still chattering as we crossed the bridge. I
couldn't believe how rude she was acting- and I could tell that Jared
was really starting to become irritated by her.

But over the top of her ramblings, I thought I heard a sound
that wasn't familiar- something strange.

It sounded like some sort of creaking, or snapping, I wasn't
exactly sure.

I clomped up beside Penelope. "Shhh."

"Why? Penelope scoffed. "Do you hear Bigfoot?"

"Be quiet." I held my hand up in front of her mouth.

She slapped my hand away and said, "Don't touch me."

"No, Penelope," Jared protested. "I hear it too."

We cocked our heads towards a grove of towering cedars,

36

trying to find the curious small noise. It was a steady creaking coming from within the forest and moving steadily towards us.

"It's not an animal." I spoke low.

"No, sounds more like someone pulling an old wagon or something." Jared whispered back.

Penelope stood behind us, arms folded at her chest. "If you think you're going to scare me with your nonsense, you are sorely mistaken."

Jared rolled his eyes.

The longer we listened to the steadily increasing noise, the more we were drawn in by it. I wanted to cry out. I was terrified, but I couldn't. It had blocked out all that was familiar and safe. I could no longer hear the chattering of the Stellar Jays that perched in the vine maples, or the groan of Mr. Massingale's generator. The calming melody of water rushing over stone had left me. All I could do was listen.

Penelope heard it now too, and had moved behind Jared, grasping his t-shirt. "Do you think it *could* be Bigfoot?" She whispered.

"Well," Jared mused. "I suppose it could be. But if it is, I think he needs to oil his knee caps."

I couldn't help but smirk.

The salmonberry bushes started to rustle, and I felt my throat go dry. I pointed.

"Well," Jared's voice cracked. "It looks like whoever, or whatever is coming out to say hello."

Penelope screamed at the top of her lungs. The sound scattered the Stellar Jays and pierced the cloudless sky.

A frail figure emerged from the forest. She had long white hair that hung loose around her shriveled face. She wore a long heavy skirt of purple wool with a tan men's dress shirt neatly tucked in. To finish the ensemble, she wore a long white apron tied neatly around her waist and a floppy straw hat crowned her head. She was rolling a rusty wheelbarrow full of weeds.

I recognized her. It was old Ms. Stella, the witch who lived on the edge of Willow Creek, the witch who had saved my life.

Over the years- so many stories had been told about her. One of the stories was of a man, whose wayward wife had paid Ms. Stella to put a curse on him. He got angry and cut out Ms. Stella's tongue. After he took care of her, the man took his wife to the river, tied himself to her and jumped- drowning them both. After that, old Ms. Stella went crazy. It had been told to me, by a reliable source, that she could put a hex on you just by looking into your eyes. I squeezed my eyes shut. I was not about to be hexed.

"Good afternoon Master Jared- young ladies."

I peered with one eye. *Wait a minute*; I thought to myself, *she talks*. Katie Winslow was so going to get it for telling me that story.

"You gave us quite a fright, Ms. Stella," Jared said.

"So I heard." She settled her wheel barrel onto the pavement. "Now," she mused. "Did that scream come from the dark beauty on your left or from fair Olivia on your right?"

"It was Penelope." Jared stepped aside, exposing Penelope. She immediately puffed up and crossed her arms. She reminded me of our old rooster who used to puff up and madly flap his wings every time you came close to the hen house. But I could see right through her bluff just like I could see through the roosters. She, like the rooster, trembled.

Stella smiled, exposing surprisingly white teeth for someone, who looked to me to be about 150 years old. "Well," she said. "Miss Penelope you may want to gargle with a little honey and lemon tonight to soothe that throat. I imagine it will be a little sore. You gave it quite a workout."

"Looks like a nice batch of nettles." Jared poked at her cargo, stinging himself on one of the finely haired, but potent leaves. He rubbed his finger.

"Nettle tea," she remarked. "Good for the body and soul." She smiled. "Well Jared, tell your mom I'll be by soon to check up on her."

"Okay, I will. It was nice to see you again."

Ms. Stella lifted the handles of the small broken down wheelbarrow with its load of nettles, and we watched as she creaked down the road to the dusty drive that ran along Willow Creek.

"What freak show did that old hag escape from?" Penelope sarcastically asked.

"She's not a freak," I interjected. "She's a witch."

"She's not a freak and she is definitely not a witch." Jared shook his head and walked up the road. We both followed. "She's a very nice person," he continued, "and very smart. I'll bet you didn't know it, but she's a doctor. She was an obstetrician in Seattle for 30 years. Fifteen years ago she visited this area and it changed her life. She gave up her practice, sold her apartment, and bought the cottage on Willow Creek. She told my parents she was finally at peace with herself."

Jared stopped to take advantage of a breeze that had picked up. He lifted his face into it and closed his eyes. The breeze ruffled his hair- lifting it from around his face. "She's become a well respected naturopathic," he added, dreamily opening his eyes. "Some moron started a rumor that she had had her tongue cut out. Can you believe there are idiots in this community who actually believe that nonsense?" He smiled right at me.

"Okay," Once again, I felt the need to explain something I should've just let go. "So maybe, yeah, I've heard the story," I said. "But, I never believed it." I looked at the road. I *was* a rotten liar.

"Still, I heard you call her a witch." He turned his attention to Penelope. He looked straight into her large dark eyes. "You passed judgment on her before she drew a breath. I would think of all people, you would understand. Now you're guilty of the same crime you're so afraid of being committed to you."

Penelope took her defensive position- crossed arms over puffed out chest. "And what crime is that Mr. Know-It-All?"

"Being judged. You're afraid of being made fun of because you don't feel you fit into the mold." He paused for a moment. "That's why you brag so much and are so snappy with everyone. You try to cover up your insufficiencies with mock sophistication, but you're not fooling anyone. You're insecure."

Penelope spoke through gritted teeth. "Jared, you don't know anything." I could tell she knew he spoke the truth. I had heard her say it earlier on the phone. She glanced at me quickly, and then looked at the ground.

"I do know that you saw an old lady in a long skirt, pushing a rusty wheelbarrow today, and immediately she became a freak in your eyes."

She became defensive again. "I'm so sorry that an old lady wearing weird clothes and pushing a wheelbarrow appearing from out of nowhere seems odd to me. Please, I beg you, forgive me."

He chuckled. "Look," he said. "What if I had told you my mom knew a retired doctor from Seattle, who is living in the area now. Her name is Stella, and she's studying the medicinal properties of wild native plants. Would you have thought of her as a freak then?"

Neither Penelope nor I had a thing to say. No wonder he thought I was an immature idiot. I was.

He shrugged. "Don't judge a book by its cover."

By this time, we had all grown weary of our walk. I know I felt completely beaten down, both by the heat and Jared's words. I wondered what else could possibly happen to me that day. If it hadn't been for that one bright pinprick of light, when Jared commented on my hair, this would have gone down as one of the worst days of my life.

By the scowl on Penelope's face, I could tell it hadn't exactly been a four star day for her either. But then again, I doubted if any day was.

"Shall we turn back?" Jared asked.

We both shook our heads, and slowly followed his lead back towards Willow Creek.

We walked in silence. The only sounds, the clip, clop of my cowboy boots on pavement and the occasional curious insect buzzing around our faces.

We were just about to cross back over the Willow Creek bridge when we heard-

"Yoo- Hoo! Hey kids!"

"Who's the Swiss miss with the fat stomach," Penelope blurted.

I squinted to make out who it was. Waddling toward us in a pale blue sundress was Diane Wahl. Her braids dangled like ropes from underneath a straw gardening hat.

"That's Jared's mom," I said. "She's not fat, she's going to have a baby. And by the way-" I quickly added, "She's not Swiss."

Jared started laughing.

"What's so funny?" I asked.

"Well," he smirked. "Actually, she is half Swiss."

Penelope gave me a satisfied- "Hmpf."

"Oh, come on Penelope, You couldn't tell she was Swiss. You were making fun of her braids."

"You'll never know." She managed to whisper before Diane caught up with us.

"I was wondering if I'd run into you guys," Jared's mom said, breathless.

She gently took hold of my braid. "Hey Livvy," she said, and gave it a gentle tug. "Jared didn't mention you were walking too."

Jared started to explain, "Well, Penelope doesn't like to..."

But before anymore could be added, I said, "This is my cousin, Penelope."

"Yes." Diane said, reaching out a soil stained hand. "It's nice to meet you."

Penelope smiled so sweetly- she practically dripped. She took her hand, and said, "It's so nice to meet you."

Man, I have never seen anyone able to change faces the way Penelope could. She was a real chameleon. One minute snarly and horrid, the next minute, she was as sweet as twenty-five cent candy.

"Oh Jared," his mom turned to him. "Penelope is every bit as lovely as you described."

I could tell Jared's mom had made him feel uncomfortable. "Yeah, thanks Mom," he mumbled, then scooped up a handful of pebbles and started tossing them into the creek.

I have to admit I was somewhat bothered by the comment. It annoyed me to think of Jared rushing home that morning to tell his mom all about Livvy's *pretty* cousin. As if he couldn't believe someone as ugly as me was capable of being related to someone as pretty as her.

Diane Wahl decided to switch gears; I think to save her son from any more embarrassment. So, she turned her attention on me.

"Livvy," she said. "I've been meaning to ask you something."

"Oh sure, you can ask me anything." I answered. And that was where I made my mistake. If I had only said something like- No, I'm not taking questions today. Or maybe- It's against my religion to answer questions on Wednesdays, I would have been safe. But, no I said, '*Oh sure, you can ask me anything.*'

"You'll be 13 soon, right?" She continued.

"Yeah, in a couple weeks," I said. "My mom has a big bash planned for me. My dad will be home too. I'm really excited" I proceeded to tell her about the cake and the decorations and the fireworks. She smiled so sweetly as I chattered on about my party; it was as if we had connected in some familiar way. I almost felt as if we were part of the same family- but then she had to go and blow it.

She used eight words- eight harmless, little words that have little meaning on their own, but when she placed them in the right order, those same eight words, spewed upon me like vomit.

"So Livvy, have you started your cycle yet?"

I stared at her blankly. I hoped she wasn't asking me what, in my heart, I knew she was.

"You know," she continued, "your menstrual cycle."

"Yeah," I cleared my throat. "I know what you mean." That tiny bright pinprick of light that had been the saving grace for this day had just been puttied over by Diane Wahl. I was mortified. I didn't look at Jared to see his reaction. In fact, I had pretty much assumed that there was no possible way I could ever manage to be in his presence again. I didn't need to glance in Penelope's direction. The sound of her smirk was enough to let me know she was enjoying this.

"I'm sorry." She put her arm around my shoulder. "I didn't mean to embarrass you."

"Oh, no," I squeaked. "You didn't embarrass me." I forced a weak smile.

"Well, it's just that I was hoping to host a full moon party for you."

"Hey Livvy," Penelope had to get her dig in. "That sounds like fun. Mrs. Wahl, could you explain to us exactly what a full moon party is." Sarcasm dripped from every syllable. I hated her.

"Well Penelope, She rubbed her belly as she talked. "It's a party given to a girl entering womanhood. We come together and welcome her with advice and gifts. We share a wonderful meal and present her with a moon journal. A moon journal is used to write about the newly found emotions that come with this new season of life." She stopped to reflect for a moment, and then started to play with my braid. "When a girl starts her cycle, it's like the door to womanhood has been opened. She is transformed. You see, each cycle of the moon, one seed will ripen and flow forth…"

"Okay, I interrupted and pulled away. "Look at the time!" Since I wasn't wearing my watch, in desperation, I glanced towards the sun. "Penelope and I were supposed to be home by now. We have to help with dinner." I grabbed Penelope by the arm and pulled her down the road with me. I didn't look back. The last thing I wanted etched into my memory was the expression on Jared's face as I discussed my blossoming womanhood with his mom.

"Tell your mom I'll call her so we can discuss the details of your full moon party," she called out. "It was nice to meet you Penelope!"

"Bye," Penelope said, laughing.

When we finally got home, I stormed directly into the kitchen, where my mom was slicing potatoes for dinner.

She smiled and started to say something, but I cut her off. "Mom," I said. "If Diane Wahl calls and mentions anything about a full moon. Just say no." With that, I stormed out and cradled myself in the arms of my favorite tree.

"When you know better you do better."
Maya Angelou

Chapter 1

For two weeks Penelope and I managed to avoid each other.

Mom tried her hardest to get us to do things together. One day, she went as far as to assign us chores to do together.

She stood under the jamb of our front door with her giant straw bag hanging off one shoulder. She handed me one of two lists she held in her right hand.

"What's this for?" I questioned.

"I want all of the chores I have listed on that piece of paper done before I get home." She paused. "Do we need ketchup? I don't think I have that written down." She checked the list she was holding.

"It says here to wash Dad's truck." I grimaced. "Why do I have to do that? He hasn't been home to get it dirty."

"It's been dry." She fumbled through her giant bag, looking for a pencil. "It's covered with dust. I want it clean before he gets home this weekend. Speaking of clean," she found a pencil and was busily scribbling ketchup onto her list. "I want that braid out of your hair and that mop washed."

"Fine." I rolled my eyes.

"Penelope."

Penelope was sitting in the recline position of my dad's barca lounger. "Yes, Aunt Claire." She closed her book gingerly over her hand to save her place.

"This list is for you too. Your parents asked me to keep you busy."

"Of course I'll help." She opened her book and continued to read.

"Can you think of anything else I'm forgetting?" Mom was shuffling through her bag again. I don't know why, but when ever she thinks she's forgetting something, or missing something, she digs in that giant straw bag. Granted, it is big enough to garage a small car.

"No." I said, blandly.

"I'll be back around three. Diane knows you're here and will probably be calling to check in on you."

"Happy shopping." I said, and stood watching until she backed the jeep out of the drive. She honked as she sped away.

The day was already tired. Everything drooped and it wasn't even noon yet. I used to think that I would love to live somewhere like California, where it was hot and dry most of the time. But that day, looking out across the sun-baked yard, I began to think differently. I missed the rain. There's a rustling that happens before an approaching storm-waves of movement. And if you listen to the rustling long enough, you can almost hear the trees say- *it's coming- it's coming*! Then right before the first big plops, a sweet, fresh fragrance perfumes the air.

'*If they found a way to bottle this up*, my grandma used to say. *I'd wear it all the time.*' I used to think that was a dumb thing to say. But that day, I wouldn't have minded wearing a little of that perfume myself.

"Don't even think you're going to get out of helping me today, Penelope." I turned back into the house to confront her. She was gone. "Go ahead and hide, but I'm telling Mom!"

I felt a tap on my shoulder. I turned and Penelope stood poised, waving a twenty-dollar bill in front of my face. I eagerly pulled the bribe from her manicured fingers and stuffed it into the pocket of my cut-offs, before padding out the back door to find a bucket and a sponge.

The next day, Mom found the twenty-dollar bill in the pocket of my soiled cut-offs while she was doing laundry. We confessed, and mom put the money in an envelope saying neither of us deserved it. She drove us into town, and made us go into the animal shelter.

Mrs. Dickerson thought we were just the sweetest little things for donating our hard earned money to the shelter. She gave us both a cookie. Homemade, of course.

Later that afternoon, Katie called.

"Hey- I was wondering if you were alive. You haven't even tried to call me," she said.

"I'm sorry," I said. "It's just been a little weird around here. My cousin Penelope is here for the summer. Needless to say, I'm not exactly pleased."

"Well, how bout if I come over and spend the night? We can ride horses and goof around at-"

I cut her off. ""I don't think so. Like I said, it's just been too weird around here and besides, you remember what happened last time you spent the night while Penelope was here. You totally embarrassed me."

"Livvy, I was ten when that happened, just a child. I'm twelve now, and perfectly capable of controlling myself. Did the stain ever come out?"

"No."

"Oh."

"Okay." I gave in. "You can spend the night, but under the conditions that you do not speak to Penelope and you do not drink grape juice."

"I'll have mom drop me off at six."

I hung up the phone and took a bite of the sandwich I had successfully completed while talking with my friend. As I chewed, feelings of forebode wrapped around me like an old wool blanket-scratchy and hot. I swallowed; gagging slightly on peanut butter, then immediately used the sprayer at the kitchen sink to cool myself down. I had decided it was an omen. Something bad was going to happen.

My mom came into the kitchen. She was carrying a load of

clean dishtowels and humming a tune I recognized from a Celtic CD she likes.

She stared at me for the longest time. "Do I need to get my eyes checked, or is my daughter showering with the sink sprayer in the middle of our kitchen?"

I didn't know exactly what to say. "I had a hot flash," fell clumsily from my lips.

Mom put the towels on the butcher block. "What is wrong with you lately. These are not the actions of the daughter I have been raising for almost 13 years." She pointed to the water soaked floor.

"Well, I think something bad is going to happen. I invited Katie over-"

"Wait a minute," she interrupted. "You invited someone over without asking me?"

"Well," I tried to explain. Water dripped off my hair and into my eyes. I rubbed them, irritating them more. "She kind of invited herself over, and I couldn't just say no. Besides, after I got off the phone, I think I felt an omen coming on and I had to spray myself."

She didn't look convinced. "What are you talking about?" she paused. "Omen?"

"Well, I just got all hot, then I gagged on my sandwich, and I had to spray myself because I thought I was going to suffocate."

"Maybe you felt hot because it's 90 degrees outside and your wearing over-alls." She stared at me a little longer, making me feel completely uncomfortable. "Tell you what I'm going to do. I'm going to leave this room." She smiled. "Then let's say, in 30 minutes, I'm going to come back and this kitchen is going to be completely dry, and you will be busy watering the vegetable and flower gardens."

"Fine," I said. "Can Katie and I ride horses when she gets here?"

"Not unless you plan on inviting Penelope too."

"Fine, we'll find something else to do."

"You better include Penelope." Her voice was an octave higher than usual.

"Fine." I was done. Mom was in a lousy mood; I shouldn't have tried to talk with her at all. She always got a little nervous a couple days before daddy got home, but that day her sense of humor must of gotten accidentally shuffled with the junk in her giant bag. Usually she doesn't mind if Katie comes over uninvited. And as for the water mess, it was just water for goodness sake. She didn't have to have a fit over it. Oh well, the rest of day I would be confined to a watering can and hose. I knew I felt an omen.

"It's not what you look at that matters, it's what you see."
Henry David Thoreau

Chapter 8

Katie Winslow was a frail brunette, who had lived with childhood asthma until she turned 10. So instead of getting attention by excelling in sports or dance or even academics, Katie excelled in gossip. Once she got hold on a story, she liked to spread it. Like viruses, her tales would slightly mutate as they spread from student to student throughout the school. By the time the stories came full circle, you hardly recognized them, and there was usually no cure for the damage they would sometimes create. Needless to say, I was Katie's only real friend.

Katie arrived at my house promptly at six. She was breathless and chatty. "Guess who was caught kissing Joshua Lee," she said, waving as her mother drove away.

"Who?" I tucked her sleeping bag under my arm.

She smiled. "Lizzy."

"No!" I stopped dead in my tracks, dropping her sleeping bag onto one of mom's daylilies. I tucked it back under my arm, quickly checking to see if Mom had witnessed the accidental assault. "Lizzy?" I questioned. "The shyest girl in the whole school? Are you sure?"

She shook her head.

"What would she be doing with Joshua? He's a total jock, and she's such a book worm."

"I'm telling you, it's true. Noah told me about it. He saw them kissing on a bench at the mall in Mt. Vernon. He said he was with his mom in the book store when he looked up from a copy of Captain Underpants, and there they were kissing on a bench in front of the shoe store." She thought for a moment. "Well, okay, he did say the mall was really crowded, but he was absolutely sure that it was Joshua and Liz."

"I don't know Katie, I can't picture them together. Oh, by the way," I stopped at the bottom of the porch steps.

"What?"

I balled up my fist and punched her in the shoulder.

"Ouch!" She said, rubbing her shoulder, and giving me her evil eye. "What was that for?"

"That was for that stupid story you told me six years ago about Ms. Stella, the witch. Thanks to you, and Jared's mom, I looked like a complete idiot in front of Jared."

"I don't know what you're talking about."

"I saw Stella. She talks."

"Oh my gosh! Livvy, did she hex you?" She grabbed my shoulders and tried fixate on my pupils. "Have you been hexed? You know, if you throw salt over your shoulder and walk around an old oak three times, I think it can be reversed." She started to drag me up the porch steps. "I wish I were more sure about the cure. We gotta look this up on the internet."

"Katie!" I pushed her away. "She didn't hex me. She was nice."

"Oh, she hexed you all right." Katie continued pulling me up the stairs. "It's okay, after I fix you up, everything will come back."

I couldn't help but laugh. "Come on Katie, let's go in the house and harass my cousin."

"So, when were you with Jared?"

"Never mind!"

Katie and I trudged up the staircase dragging her sleeping bag and backpack behind us.

We met Penelope at the top. She had been up in her room most of the afternoon, I had supposed, she spent her time staring at herself in the mirror.

"Do you remember Katie?" I asked Penelope.

She looked Katie up and down. You're the twerp who vomited the grape juice all over my white cashmere sweater two years ago.

"You remember me!" Katie seemed thrilled that someone as cool as Penelope would give her recognition for anything, even something as disgusting as puking grape juice all over her.

"How could I forget." She parted us with graceful hands, as if she were Moses, and we were the red sea, walking between us and down the stairs and into the kitchen.

"Your cousin is the most beautiful girl I have ever seen." Katie sighed, as she watched her. "I would give anything to be like her. Wouldn't you?"

I stuck my finger right in my friend's face. "If you want to sleep in my room, stupid questions like that better not escape your lips again." I poked her nose, and went into my room, throwing her sleeping bag onto the floor.

I lie upon the rumpled covers on my bed. It made me mad that Katie worshiped Penelope. It ticked me off the way Jared cooed over her two weeks before. And it really annoyed me the way my own mother expected me to entertain her- like I was some sort of prancing poodle.

I heard my bedroom door creak open. I looked up. Katie was standing in the doorway. She looked like a pixie that had lost her wings.

"I didn't mean to hurt your feelings." She said, giving me a half smile.

She looked so pathetic; I couldn't help but forgive her.

"It's okay, Katie." I sat up. "Sorry I poked you, but do see the stress she puts me through?" I threw myself back onto the bed.

"Well," Katie said. She sat next to me. "She does have pretty big feet for someone her size."

I sat up again. "You know," I said. "Her feet are big. In fact, they're huge!" I know, it was pretty shallow, but it did make me feel much better. We sat on my bed for a long time that evening, making up jokes about big feet.

Mom had built a fire in the big round fire pit my dad made in the back yard. He made it from smooth round river rock we gathered from the banks of the nearby Skagit River.

He had also built four benches that were situated in a circular pattern around the fire pit.

My family could be found out there most pleasant evenings roasting a wiener on the end of a freshly broken alder branch over a crackling fire.

The smoke from the fire would sometimes snake around our faces- burning our eyes and throats. Without a second thought, we would rotate to the next smoke free bench. Round and round we'd go, our own game of musical chairs, except nobody realizes they're playing.

Mom, Katie and I were already roasting our hot dogs when Penelope found her way to the fire pit. She stood back grimacing as she watched mom throw another log into the pit. The fire coughed a plume of smoke that rose and snaked its way towards Penelope.

"Is that smoke going to permeate my clothing?" She asked Mom.

"Oh honey, is that an expensive outfit?"

She shook her head.

"Did you bring any play clothes?"

"I don't own any play clothes."

"Hmm." My mom thought for a moment. "I've got it! Go into the utility room- on top of the dryer are a pair of gray, patched sweat pants and a red t-shirt. While you're here, those will be your official play clothes." Mom smiled.

Maybe it was the way the fire reflected off of Penelope's features, but she looked stressed, like maybe wearing my play clothes was the equivalent of walking around with dog poop on her shoe. She sucked in her breath and looked at me.

"Go ahead," I said. "In fact, you can have them. I'm sure the patched butt will impress all the girls at dance class."

"Thank you," she said, glancing back at Mom. She turned and disappeared into the darkness.

Mom waited until Penelope was out of ear shot before- "Olivia

Adrienne Smith!" She used my full name, that meant she was ticked! "What is wrong with you?"

"What did I do?"

"You have been treating Penelope like dirt."

"Oh," I interrupted. "You should hear how she talks to me when you're not around. I'm telling you Mom- she's evil!" I felt like I was about to cry. I closed my eyes and took a breath. "She's totally playing you and you don't even know it." I concluded in almost a whisper.

"Oh, Olivia honey," my mom's voice had softened. "I'm not stupid. Have you ever heard of a third eye?"

I looked at her. The fire had begun to burn hot- shooting sparks into the night sky and casting an amber glow upon her face. "Yeah, I've heard you talk about it about a million times," I said, rolling my eyes.

"Well, when you become a parent you'll grow one."

Katie's eyes widened. "Grow one? Where?"

"Right here on the back of your head." Mom parted the back of her hair.

Katie started to lean over to see, but I tugged on her sweatshirt before she was completely made a fool of.

"I'm teasing you, Katie." Mom reached over and patted her shoulder. "No, you will not literally grow a third eye. It's more like an extra sense." She thought for a moment. "A mom sense." Mom turned and grabbed my hand. "I know exactly how she's acting, and I know why she's doing it. She is uncomfortable and her snootiness and bragging are just, well, a defense mechanism." She paused. "You need to treat her just like you would Katie or any other friend. You'll see, if you ignore it she'll be fine." She glanced at her wiener she had been roasting. "Oh, No! I think it's a little over done." She laughed.

Mom pulled what looked like a black cigar off the end of her branch and tossed it back into the fire. We watched as the flames enveloped it- shrinking and twisting it until it disintegrated.

"What's so interesting?" Penelope had changed into my sweats and was looking curiously into the fire.

Katie's eyes twinkled. "We're watching a wiener burn," she

said.

"Oh, how entertaining."

"Penny." My mom leaned towards her. "There are branches leaning against the picnic table. I want you to grab one and also take a wiener out of the Tupperware container.
You will then put the wiener on the stick and cook it over the fire. After that, you take the cooked wiener back to the picnic table and put it into a bun. Then you can use the condiments to dress it with."

Penelope smiled. "It's called a hot dog- right?"

"I'm sorry! I didn't mean to patronize you."

"No, it's okay Aunt Claire, this actually will be the first time I've cooked one on a-" she paused and picked up the gnarled alder branch. "Well, a stick. We usually grill them."

"Well, see," my mom, said. "We learn something new everyday."

I watched Penelope walk uncomfortably with her branch and wiener. I thought it odd how different she looked wearing my clothes. She had transformed from a cocky 19 year old wanna be- back to a naïve 13 year old. She stumbled over a rock as she found her way to the empty bench across the fire from me.

I watched her fumble trying to get the slippery dog onto the branch for several minutes.

"Oh, goodnight!" I finally said. "You're making me nervous with that thing. Let me help you."

Mom touched my arm and gave me one of her approving winks as I marched around the fire pit.

"Scoot." I said to Penelope.

She moved over- surrendering to me her stick and wiener.

"Okay, I find the best way to secure this thing," I said. "Is to poke the stick vertically through the middle of the dog." I slid the stick into the bottom end of the wiener. "You have to get it at least half way through," I continued. "Or the stupid wiener will just break off into the fire. Well, Okay." I handed her the branch. "You are ready to roast."

She looked straight at me. "Thank you," she said.

Now, I wasn't sure if I was imagining things, but I thought we had connected. She didn't jump up and down or give me a high five.

She didn't even smile, but there was something in her eyes. A softening.

"You're welcome." I said, and moved quickly back to my bench.

"Well, I'm going in," mom stood and stretched. "Remember to douse that fire before you kids come in."

"We know, Mom. We're not babies you know." I teased her.

"Isn't it nice to know you're loved." She mussed my hair before gingerly wandering off. "Goodnight you three," echoed from out of the darkness.

We sat quietly around the fire. Katie found her way to the marshmallows. She popped a couple in her mouth followed by a square of chocolate and finally piece of graham cracker. She looked like chipmunk.

"You have no idea how absolutely annoying I find it when you do that." I said to Katie.

"Humph, humph" She mumbled, pointing to her full cheeks.

"What?"

She swallowed. "I said, you know how I hate hot marshmallows." Then she popped two more marshmallows into her mouth followed by another square of chocolate and by more graham cracker. She smiled and marshmallow oozed from the corners of her mouth.

"Okay. You're making me sick." I said, changing benches to escape the smoke of our dwindling fire.

She laughed and marshmallow and chocolate drooled down her face.

"SICK!" I yelled. I picked up a handful of grass and moss from the ground. "It looks like someone needs her face washed," I said, charging at her.

"No!" she squealed, as I rubbed grass and moss into her marshmallow covered face. We both fell to the ground, laughing. I was still laughing when I glanced to where Penelope was sitting. She was gone. "I wonder where she went?" I said, looking around.

"She probably got sick of your childishness." Katie said, picking moss and grass out the marshmallow and chocolate goop covering her face.

"Very funny." I plopped down in the grass and watched the gibbous moon rise above the tree line, while Katie silently threw twigs to the dying flames of our fire. And all the while the never-ending song of croaking frogs played in the background.

"I wonder what she told Mom we were doing?" I broke the silence.

"Who?" Katie answered.

I looked behind me to where she was sitting. "Penelope, of course."

"Oh. I'll bet she didn't even talk to your mom."

"I'm sure she did. She either told on us because we were being disgusting, or she told on us because we weren't including her." I laid my head onto the grass. "Either way, I'm in trouble."

"I'm sure she just went to take a shower or whatever."

"Yeah, you're right. She probably went in to wash the smoke off herself before it *permeated* her skin."

"Then again," Katie continued. "She could have went in to tell on us for being both disgusting and not including her and then you get into double trouble.

I sighed. "Thanks, Katie."

"Not a problem."

Katie got up to graze the picnic table again. As for me, I watched the swelling moon and thought of Diane Whal.

A blood curdling scream came from the house startling me up to a sitting position and silencing the frogs.

"Oh my gosh!" Katie dropped a bag of chips. "What was that?"

I stood up and grabbed the pocketknife from the picnic table my mom had used to cut the branches with. "I don't know, but I am definitely freaked-out."

Katie was hugging up behind me. "Do you think your cousin could have flipped out and tried to kill your mom?" she whispered.

"With what?" I asked. "Her fingernail file?"

We heard another scream, followed by what sounded like a man's laugh.

"There's somebody in the house." Katie said, shrinking behind me.

My heart was pounding in my throat. I couldn't believe this was happening to us. This was like something you read about in magazines or watched on late night television. These kinds of things didn't happen to us. Not here.

Katie was whimpering behind me and my legs were rubber bands, but I had to do something. "Mama!" I yelled out. "Penelope!" I started running into the darkness towards the glow of the back porch light. That light had always been a beacon for me, but that night it felt more like a 'Welcome to Hell' sign.

I stumbled over every twig- every divot- as I ran. My thinking was slow and my footsteps heavy- as if the world around me had turned to porridge and I was swimming in it. The only sounds I could hear now were my short exasperated breaths and Katie calling for me to stop. But I couldn't. I had to get to my mom and my cousin. I had to help them.

That's when I ran into something large and hard- knocking me backwards and slamming the back of my head onto the grass. I opened my eyes to see a bushy haired man, his features distorted by moonlight glowering over me. I squeezed my eyes shut.

This was it. I was going to be murdered in my own backyard. A vision suddenly came to me- a flash. Katie Couric was introducing a story for one of her specials. *"Think small town life is a safe haven from the insanity of the city?"* She asks the viewing audience somberly. *"Ask the people of Cascadia, a small sleepy hamlet in the foothills of the Cascade Mountain Range in Washington State. An escaped mental patient took the area by surprise one summer's evening killing over half the residents of, the now infamous, Apple Road. Pictures of his grizzly deeds after this commercial break."*

"Livvy. Come on, Livvy girl, are you okay?"

How does this maniac know my name? I dreamily wondered. And why does he sound like my dad? "Dad!" I yelled, popping up.

"Hey, Baby. Surprise!"

I wrapped my arms around him. "Daddy," I cried. "I thought you were a serial killer."

"Your mama did too. She clocked me pretty good with one of her candle sticks."

I ran my fingers over a small red lump above his left eye. "Poor Dad. But I guess that'll teach you to warn us before you surprise us like that."

"Yeah, I think you're right." He kissed the top of my head. "Well, look who's here! How you doing, Katie?"

"You scared us. I'm going to bed." Katie marched past us with her arms folded and grass still sticking to her face.

"I apologize for that, Katie." Dad called out.

"That's okay. Welcome home." She answered, almost inaudibly. The back screen door whined as she disappeared into the house.

"So," Dad said, as we brushed past the vegetable garden. "I hear you're not too happy about Penelope being here."

"She hates me. And to be honest, the feeling is kind of mutual."

"Oh, how could anyone ever hate you?"

"Stop it, Dad. I'm serious. She treats me like I'm a pile of dog doo that she can't wait to scrape off her shoe because I don't wear expensive clothes, or take dance lessons, or eat lobster with champagne and caviar sauce *flambé*." I tried to sound French on the flambé part, but I think I came across more Slavic.

"Oh, I see." Dad was wearing a slight smile. "Have I ever told you about my friend Jimmy?"

"I don't think so."

"He's the guy your mom refers to as Bubba."

"Oh, him! The guy you go trout fishing with sometimes."

"Yeah, him. Well," Dad reflected. "Jimmy has never been married and has no children. He lives in a camper with three cats." He crinkled his nose. "You know how much I hate cats. Jimmy's never seen the ocean. But he knows every crack- every crevice and more importantly, every hidden lake in the Cascade Mountain Range." He pointed to the cragged peaks that rose in the east- towering black shadows threatening to blot out the moon.

"Oh, Bubba and me, we got nothing in common- except trout. And because of trout, ole Bubba has touched my life."

"How can some weird guy with cats *touch* your life?

"With his stories, Livvy girl. See, me and Jimmy have

something you and Penelope don't have."

"And what's that?" I was starting to think Dad's story was lame.

"R-E-S-P-E-C-T." He scuffled the top of my hair. "We listen to each other. My life has been enriched by his stories of the mountains. Through him I have seen peaks that I will never climb and have felt a kind of solitude that I would have never experienced otherwise." He snorted. "I have even enjoyed the antics of Puff-Puff, Booty and Miss Tinkle."

"Does that mean I can have a kitten now?"

"No." We both laughed.

"I don't know, Dad. It's at a point right now that I don't think I care to be *touched* by anything she has to offer." I sighed, then snapped off the tip of a cucumber vine trellising over an obelisk on the edge of the garden. "Well, I'm going to bed." I gave dad a big bear hug. "I'm so glad you're home, Daddy."

"Me too, Livvy girl," he said, and kissed the top of my forehead. "You go on in- I'm going to put some of this food away and douse what's left of that campfire."

"Thanks, Dad."

"Goodnight, Olivia, I'm sorry I scared you."

"It's okay, Dad," I said, and then climbed the back porch steps.

The house was quiet except for the faint sound of water running in the upstairs bathroom. As I climbed the staircase, I saw Mom come out of the bathroom. Steam rolled out behind her-dissipating with the cooler air. Her head was wrapped in a pale green towel and she was draped in the red and blue plaid robe she had given to Dad for Christmas two years before. He's never worn it.

"Livvy," she said, leaving a damp outline of her feet as she padded across the wide fir floorboards. "I hope your dad didn't scare you as badly as he scared me." She hugged me. The smell of lavender body wash swathed my senses, the product of a natural body and bath workshop she took in town several weeks before.

"He scared Katie more than me." I tried to sound brave. "I was on my way to see what was going on when I ran right into him."

"Well, he scared me pretty bad."

"I saw what you did to his head." I sniggered.

She smiled. Never underestimate the power of a woman."

"Yeah."

"Well, It's late, Sweetie. Don't you think you better get to bed?"

"I was just going up. Goodnight, Mama."

"Goodnight, my sweet girl." She blew a kiss to me as she padded down the steps and into the kitchen.

I silently pushed open my bedroom door. I looked through my three piles of clothes, finally spotting a clean t-shirt of Dad's and my favorite green PJ bottoms. I changed and tripped over Katie, who was softly snoring in her sleeping bag, before finally snuggling into my bed. Streaks of moonlight reached through my window, fingers of light softly touching my face. I closed my eyes and drifted off to sleep.

"The herb that can't be got is the one that heals."
Irish Saying

Chapter 9

June 21st- the longest day of the year and my birthday. Diane says being born on the summer solstice makes me special. She thinks I'm more attuned to fairy folk. I used to think she was only joking when she said stuff like that, but two years ago, on my birthday, she gave me a small envelope that contained a small sprinkling of fern seeds she had gathered at midnight. She told me if I rubbed them on my eyelids, I would see fairies. I looked to my mom who gave me her *'humor me by saying thank you'* look, which is composed of a pursed lip smile with eyes slightly pinched. Weird.

Anyway, I woke up that morning feeling good. My dad had been home a full three days and Penelope had come down with a stomach virus, which had kept her in her room. I was hoping she would stay sick long enough to miss my party. The last thing I needed was for my smarty-pants cousin to embarrass me by being rude to my friends at my 13th birthday party.

I bounded down the stairs that morning. The smoky aroma of bacon frying clung to the air. "Ahh," I stopped short of the kitchen to breath in its smoky goodness.

"I can't believe she said that to Livvy. Poor, Livvy. She must have felt humiliated." I overheard my dad talking in the kitchen.

"Oh, Steve, you should have seen the look on the poor child's face when she came in the house." My mom answered. "She came running into the kitchen and said to me- *Mom, if Diane says anything about a moon, just say no-* then she burst out the back door. Three hours later I found her sitting in the arms of a tree down by the slough. That's where she finally told me the whole story."

My parents were discussing what had happened with Diane Wahl. I decided to become small and listen.

"Well," my dad said. "What did Diane have to say when you called her?"

"Of course, she felt terrible." Mom was mixing something as she talked. Waffle batter. It was a tradition for us to have bacon and waffles with fresh fruit and whip cream on my birthday. "I explained to Diane," my mom continued, "that the gesture was nice. It was just that we felt bringing up something as delicate as a menstrual cycle in front of Jared and Penny was not appropriate."

"Well, obviously, it's not appropriate! What was that woman thinking?"

"Steve, honey, she's known Livvy since she was born. She thinks of her as a daughter. I suppose it felt right. Anyway, she wants to apologize. I told her that would be great, but not to do it in front of Livvy's friends."

I didn't even know my mom had called her. She never told me anything about it. I smiled to myself. I felt like a small bird in the safety of the nest. I felt protected.

I decided it was a good time to make my entrance. I burst through the door. "Is this not a glorious morning?"

"Good morning, birthday girl," Mom said, brightly. "Are you ready for your birthday breakfast?"

"Wow! 13 years old. Just think, Claire, in 3 short years, Livvy will be driving."

Mom dropped the spoon she was mixing with into the bowl. I watched it being swallowed by the thick, creamy waffle batter. She placed her hand over her mouth and started to sniffle.

Dad and I just looked at each other. "Claire, you

okay?" My dad asked.

"Just ignore me. My baby's growing up- that's all."

I didn't know what to say. It wasn't my fault I was growing up. "I'm sorry, Mom."

"It's not your fault, she said, wiping her eyes. "Time marches on and I need to learn to deal with it. Oh no! My spoon!" She reached her hand deep into the batter and pulled out the spoon.

"Oh, that's great, Claire." My dad pointed to her hand that was gloved to the wrist with sticky waffle batter. "Just bacon and fruit for me this morning."
We all laughed.

My party was scheduled for 6:00pm, and on the longest day of the year, evening drifted in light and lovely. My dad drug out the grill and I helped mom put together vegetable, fruit and cold cut platters. We also made a huge bowl of potato salad and an even larger bowl of Caesar salad. We made Mom's famous double baked beans, corn on the cob, and shrimp cold slaw. We set out bags of corn chips and homemade salsa, and a huge cooler of soda pop.

The tables that we set up under the grape entwined pergola were basically saw horses from my dad's workshop with large sheets of plywood on top. We disguised them with Great-Grandma's beautiful cut work lace tablecloths and large bouquets made up of bright blue Delphinium spikes, soft pink old English roses, creamy white Shasta daisies, buttery clusters of Yarrow, and weaved amongst them, tendrils of English Ivy. We strung clear twinkle lights and set out torches to be lit after dark. But the piece de resistance was a gargantuan triple chocolate cake with chocolate mousse filling and covered with a thick coating of chocolate truffle frosting made especially for me by Mr. Rose over at Orchard Mill Bed and Breakfast. This was going to be a night for magic!

The only down side to the evening was that Penelope would be feeling well enough to join us. Mom had become concerned that she wasn't getting better and told her, when she brought up her lunch tray, that she would take her to see the doctor the next morning. The comment must have kick started her white blood cells, because she was up and dressed within the hour. I knew she was faking.

I dressed for the main event in a pair of clean cut-offs, my cowboy boots (with socks) and a paisley peasant top. Mom insisted she help me with my hair. I ended up with a big ponytail on the top of my head. I felt like Jeannie from that old sitcom 'I Dream of Jeannie', but Mom was right, the ponytail did keep my face cool, and my hair out of the food.

The Frostmans were the first to arrive. "I brought a relish plate," Regina Frostman was breathless as she placed a tray of artfully arranged pickles next to the potato salad.

"You didn't need to bring anything," I said, my eyes watering from the potent brine.

"Oh, Happy Birthday, Olivia!" she said, clutching me to her abundant bosom. "I could just squeeze a little blue bean from you." She pushed me harder into her soft folds. I thought I'd suffocate.

'I could just squeeze a little blue bean from you.' What was that suppose to mean anyway? She had been saying that to me since I was a toddler.

Katie and me had made a pact years ago- If she catches me at any time during my lifetime wearing permanent press slacks with the elastic waistband, walking around in public with curlers in my hair and one of those plastic rain kerchiefs tied around my chin, or saying *'I could just squeeze a little blue bean out of you,'* she is to immediately check me in to the closest mental hospital. I told her I would do the same for her. What are friends for if not to watch out for each other?

Regina released me. I gasped for air.

"Just look at you! Thirteen years old!" she said.

"Yeah, my mom cried this morning." I felt the need to say something else. Something to wow her with the sophistication that one can only gain by being thirteen. "Wow," I said. "That's a lot of pickles."

"Yes", she said, slightly lifting one end of the tray. "I have laid out my prize winning garlic dill. And these are bread and butter pickles. And these," she added, especially pleased, "are my spicy jalapeno pickles. I have also added pickled green beans and garlic." She smiled.

"Cool. Why don't I go tell Mom you're here."

"Thank you, dear. If you don't mind, I'll just make myself at home." She pointed to a lawn chair.

"Oh sure, sit. There's pop in the cooler," I said, as I trotted toward the house.

"Mom!" The back door slammed behind me. "She brought homemade pickles."

"Who brought pickles, Sweetie?" Mom was putting the finishing touches on her Green Goddess dip for the veggie tray.

"Guess?"

Mom grimaced. "I told Regina not to bring anything."

"Please tell me you're not going to make me eat a pickle in front of her. It's my birthday."

"No. Just put some on your plate and when nobody's looking toss them in the bushes."

"Okay." I smiled. Sometimes my mom's wisdom amazed me.

Stepping back outside, music filled the air. Dad had pulled out a portable CD player and the throaty offerings of Etta James softly moved amongst the guests.

I watched Tiger Swallowtail Butterflies swoop around the bouquets that dominated the tables. The Wahl twins suddenly emerged from behind the tables, jumping and grabbing at the darting butterflies. I knew the Wahls would show up which had made me nervous. I looked around, spotting Diane and Victor Wahl chatting with my dad over by the grill.

Victor Wahl was a nice guy. When I was little, he used to scare me. But what little kid wouldn't be scared when someone 6'5" topped with a crown of flaming red hair and long beard- dressed only in a canvass kilt and a pair of flip-flops- approached them with homemade fish jerky?

Though his stature and dress could be intimidating, he really was a nice guy. He was the first one over when a tree fell on the barn a few winters ago. And when the jeep broke down in the middle of the road, he thought nothing of canceling his hike with friends and running back and forth to the parts store until he and my dad got it running.

I hadn't seen Jared since the *infamous* walk. I scanned the yard and found him setting up the croquet set with David Frostman and David's creepy friend, Norton Johnson. I rolled my eyes. Who had

65

invited that kid?

"Who invited Norton Johnson?"

I jumped. "Katie! You startled me. Where'd you come from?"

"Mom dropped me off in the front. I came through the house." She handed me a small box neatly wrapped in blue tissue paper and tied with white curling ribbon.

"Thank you," I said, shaking the box. "Norton must have come with David."

"He's the creepiest guy I know. I heard he smokes two packs a day. Can you believe it? He's thirteen and already smoking two packs of cigarettes a day."

"That's so disgusting," I said, watching Norton swing a croquet mallet just short of David's big head. He ran a grubby hand through his oily hair and they both laughed.

"Come on, Katie, let's get a pop."

I put my present on a small table my mom had set up for gifts, complete with a dining room chair with a rainbow of helium balloons tied to the back of it. My makeshift birthday throne. There were already a half dozen brightly wrapped gifts on the table- most from my parents. I could tell by the pale green gingham paper. I had seen the roll sticking out of my mom's giant bag the day before.

"What kind of pop do you want?" I asked Katie.

"I don't know. What kind you got?"

We've got every kind," I said rummaging through our huge white cooler. We got grape, orange, strawberry, lemon-lime, root beer, cola." I looked at Katie and crinkled my nose. Diet cola. Yuck!"

"I'll take orange."

"Coming up!" I grabbed two orange sodas and threw one to my friend. When I stood up, I was startled to find Diane Wahl in front of me. "Oh, hi."

"Happy Birthday, Livvy. Do you think I could steal you away for just a moment?"

Oh, no! She was going to apologize to me. Why couldn't she wait? Oh, why? Oh, why? Oh, why? "Oh, sure."

"I'm sorry, Katie, I won't keep her long."

"Oh, that's okay," Katie, said. "Hannah and Tyler are here.

I'll go talk to them."

"I walked ahead of Diane to the garden shed and boosted myself up on an old painted drop leaf table mom used for potting plants, and waited for Diane to catch up. She was holding her back as she waddled toward me. A softly woven bag that draped from her shoulder swung gently as she walked.

"I need to have this baby," she said between breaths.

I laughed. "You're getting *really* big," I said, then quickly covered my mouth. Oh, great! I had just made one of those comments my mom refers to as *uncalled for*. "I'm sorry."

"Oh, no! Don't feel bad. You're right. I'm getting huge, and believe it or not, I still have eight weeks left to go." She laughed weakly.

We were silent. The big toad that lived under the potting shed lumbered out, crawling under a giant rhubarb leaf and croaking once, as if to tell us he didn't care for our presence in his domain.

Diane cleared her throat. "Well, you're probably wondering why I wanted to see you." She grabbed both of my hands. I looked into her green eyes that were flecked with gold- autumn eyes. "I just wanted to apologize to you, Olivia. I didn't mean to make you feel uncomfortable two weeks ago. I guess I wasn't thinking. I've always thought of you as one of the family, so bringing up the full moon party," she paused. "Well, I…"

"It's okay!" I interrupted. "It's actually kind of funny if you think about it." I wanted to make her feel better.

"So, I haven't done any permanent damage to your psyche?"

I shook my head.

"So, you forgive me?" She squeezed my hands.

"Of course I forgive you. I'm not mad."

"Well," she dropped my hands and reached into the small woven pack she had been carrying. "I have something for you. It's not for your birthday. I left that at the party." She handed me a package simply wrapped in brown craft paper and tied with twine. "This," she said, "is personal. I made it for you."

I unwrapped the package, neatly folding the wrapping and laying it beside me on the chipped table- then I slowly opened the small rectangular box. The earthy smell of dried lavender and rose petals tickled my nose.

"It's a moon journal," she said, satisfied. "I've been working on it for quite some time."

I pulled the book out of the box and ran my hand over the soft black velvet cover. There was a silver lame' moon stitched off to one side with the title '*Wanderings*' embroidered onto it. "This is so beautiful," I said to her. "I don't know what to say."

"Open it."

The heady smell of dried herbs was stronger- soothing.

"I made the paper for the pages myself. I mixed different flowers and herbs into the pulp. See." She flipped a couple of the oatmeal colored pages and were flecked with dried herbs. "I used Yarrow for this page. And for this one," she flipped another, "rose petals. In fact, I used yarrow, roses, lavender, lemon balm, sage, feverfew and thyme in the making of the pages."

"It's just all so beautiful. I don't know if I should write in it."

"Oh no, use it! That's what it's for." She smiled. "You know each of the plants have a meaning."

"Oh, Yeah!"

"Yeah!" She pulled on my ponytail. "But, it's up to you to figure them out. It shall be your quest, fair maiden."

I laughed as I hopped off the table. "You know, I think this is one of the best presents I have ever gotten."

"Good," she said. "Shall we head back to the party?"

"Yeah."

She tugged again on my ponytail. "Have you ever seen an old sitcom called 'I dream of Jeannie?"

"Let's not go there."

"Oh," she said, and we both laughed.

"Never, never, never give in!"
Winston Churchill

Chapter 10

*T*he party was in full throttle when we returned. Etta James was replaced with Nat King Cole. Katie was still talking with Hannah, a girl two years younger than me, with a nest of curly brown hair. Hannah and I rode horses together on occasion, sometimes stopping along the rocky banks of the Sauk River to scavenge for spherical shaped rocks. She calls the rocks 'caveman baseballs.'

Her brother, Tyler, a soft-spoken kid who was good in sports, had joined the older boys for croquet. He hung out with Joshua Lee and the other jocks at school and was a walking billboard for the Boston Red Sox.

The Yeager triplets- Angela, Heidi and Marta, had also arrived-unwitting member of what they call the freaks and losers club at school, which I used to think was a pretty funny club until I found out that Katie and I were also unsuspecting members. There they sat on a weathered garden bench, wearing matching outfits of different hues, with their legs crossed at the ankles. When they spotted me, their heads turned at the same time. "Happy Birthday, Livvy!" They said in unison, their voices so close in tone and pitch, they almost sounded as one.

I waved. "Thanks, guys! We have lots of food. Eat!"

"Thanks! We will." They said together, and then, in graceful synchronization, they strode to the pergola.

"Those girls are spooky." I said, as Katie came up beside me.

"Yeah," she said. "But that's what makes them cool."

"Yeah."

We watched them graze the buffet tables. All three took small portions of the same foods.

"I bet they're not really triplets," I said.

"What do you mean?"

"Look at them. They're clones. I bet their mother was part of some weird governmental experiment. You wait and see, one day somebody will talk and it will be all over the news." I cleared my throat and tried on my best newscaster voice. "Hundreds of sets of identical triplets born throughout the 1990s and 2000s- actually clones of their parents. Government spent millions on illegal experiments. Story at eleven."

Katie giggled. "You're so goofy."

"Yuck, they're putting pickles on their plates."

"Why do you care? Besides, I thought you liked pickles."

"Regina brought them."

"Eeww!"

"Attention!" Mom called, jangling an old cowbell she kept on the back porch rail for decoration.

Everyone stopped his or her activities. The older boys put down their croquet mallets. I watched Norton as he gently tapped his yellow ball with the side of his foot when he thought nobody was looking. It lightly rolled a couple of feet before silently coming to rest in front of one of the wickets. What a cheater.

Hannah, who had been caught up in a conversation with the Wahl twins, gently hushed them by placing a hand over each of the munchkin's mouths.

Other neighbors, who had cozied up into small groups throughout the yard lifted their heads. Old man Massingale, who I guessed had come to give his old generator a much-needed break, was involved in a heated debate with Fred Harrision. I could tell by they way he waved his hands around his head while he was talking. Fred and Barbara Harrison are friends of my parents who own a beef ranch on the other side of Willow Creek. We buy our beef from them every year. Whenever we drive by their place though, I have to look away. I feel guilty looking into the eyes of the cattle that potentially could be part of my yearly protein intake.

"Can you believe my mother?" I whispered to Katie. "I wish she wouldn't do this."

"Do what?"

"Make a big speech about me."

"It's your birthday. You're on the brink of womanhood. You deserve a big speech."

"Yeah, you're right." I smiled. My ego swelled. My head felt as tight and round as one of the helium balloons rising from my makeshift birthday throne.

"I just want to welcome you all, our friends and neighbors, to our Olivia's thirteenth birthday party," my mom called from the porch.

Everyone clapped and I lifted doe eyes to my admiring friends and neighbors. "Here she goes." I said, as Katie nudged me.

"Yes," Mom continued. "They grow up way too fast." She stopped to regain her vanishing composure. "But before I start crying, I want to take the time to introduce another very special young lady who has come to share the summer with us."

Penelope slid gracefully from around the door sparkling in hot pink Capri pants and white tee shirt. She had her raven silk hair rolled into a graceful knot as a crown.

"This is Penelope Smith, our niece." Mom grabbed her hand. "While her parents are touring Europe, she has graciously agreed to be our guest. So, I want everyone to help her feel welcome."

And that was that. The speech was over. Everyone clapped, except me. Mom disappeared into a small sea of ladies, who proceeded to compliment her on the party. As for Penelope, she tried to sneak back into the house, but before she got through the door, Regina Frostman touched her shoulder. As for me, I felt rejected. Penelope had managed to wriggle her way to center stage once again.

"So, honey," Regina said, taking Penelope's hand and leading her down the porch steps. "What's it like to be the daughter of a famous model?"

Penelope smiled half-heartedly. "I suppose it feels the same as being the daughter of any woman who works hard."

"You're definitely not the same as anybody else, dear." Regina patted her hand, before joining the other ladies.

Penelope blinked before wandering to a lawn chair.

Evening drifted into a moon filled night. Candles were lit and shadows danced, but no fairies that night. We had eaten our fill and played stupid games. I self consciously opened my gifts to many courteous *"oohs"* and *"ahhs."* Mom and Dad had given me everything on my list: a compass, new pocketknife, camp light and a digital camera. Dad made the shady comment that the camera would be useful for the *whole family*. Just as suspected- an alternative motive to their generous gift. I had a feeling my camera would very soon be disappearing into Mom's giant bag.

The Yeager triplets gave me a t-shirt that said 'ex-princess' on it. Katie had wrapped a gift card because she says I never like what she gets me. Well, she'd always get me impractical things like fancy hair ties or trendy jewelry. Dust collectors.

Everybody else gave me cards with cash. I collected $75.00 all together. Oh, except for the Wahls. The Wahls gave me a medicine bag with some sort of dog hair and corn in it. Diane said I'd thank her one-day.

But even the gifts didn't spark me. What had happened to my night of magic? My grand awakening? Even with the ball of a moon glowing over us like a Chinese lantern, I felt numb. Mom's stupid *welcome Penelope to my daughter's party* speech had ruined everything.

I had decided to wander into the house because I knew where the good ice cream was hidden. Ben and Jerry's New York Super Chunk was hidden behind a pound of hamburger in the left hand side of the freezer and I could hear it whispering my name. I pulled it out of the freezer and ate it directly out of the carton.

Irish music tangled with voices and laughter poured through the open back door. Mom was going to step dance. She wasn't exactly 'Riverdance' material, but she wasn't half bad either. She had learned it from an Irish great-aunt and had tried to teach me. I was all feet and knees- tripping and clunking. She gave up.

I heard the whine of the front screen door. Thinking it was

Katie, I took the pint container and started for the living room, but stopped short of the kitchen door when I heard David's voice.

"I about dropped dead when I saw Olivia's cousin. She is hot!" David said, creepily.

Figures, I thought and shoved another chocolaty spoonful into my mouth.

"Too bad she's black." Norton snorted.

"Well, she's only half." David added.

"I don't care how white her rich little daddy is. She's as dark as chocolate, my friend, and in my book that makes her a freak." Norton said, smugly.

"I'd say she was more of a zebra." David laughed.

Dark chocolate ice cream pooled on my tongue; I was unable to swallow. I spat the ice cream back into the container before exploding into the living room to the surprise of David and Norton.

"How dare you!" I screamed. "How dare you judge Penelope by the color of her skin! Our we still living the dark ages here?" I was shaking with anger. Anger that had boiled up from the deepest part of my being, practically melting the ice cream still in my hand. "The both of you should be ashamed! I would consider myself lucky if I were half the person she is," I stammered. "She's smart and graceful and beautiful. And yes, she has beautiful dark skin that won't get all wrinkled like your pasty, pimply faces will." I stopped to catch my quickening breath. "She's human." I choked out. "What else matters?"

Norton stared at me, unmoved by my passionate outbreak. "You know, Livvy, everyone at school thinks you may be psycho." He sneered. "Now I have proof. You are psycho."

David chuckled. "Let's go, Norton before she breaks into song."

I threw the half melted container of ice cream at them as they bolted out the front door, missing them completely and leaving our screen door splattered with chocolate and nuts.

I stood. Silence enveloped me and I collapsed in a pool of tears at the bottom of our wide fir staircase. I had been a fool. I hated Penelope for a lot of reasons but not one of them had anything to do with the color of her skin. If nothing else I was jealous of her because of the color of her skin. She was beautiful. She was graceful. She was smart. She was confident. I was not. It all came down to jealousy. I was ashamed. Not only of David and Norton for their ignorance, but of myself. I had let jealousy turn me into a fool.

That's when I felt a hand lightly touching my back. I was startled and sat up stiffly. It was Penelope.

"I was at the top of the stairs," she said, quietly. "I saw the whole thing."

I didn't say anything. I just looked at her and sobbed. She kneeled down beside me and took my hand. "When I was a little girl," she said, "I was at dance class, and my instructor handed me some paperwork, which I was suppose to take home and have my mom fill out. Well, Mom was running late that day, so I decided to fill out the paperwork myself. As I sat in the empty office of the dance academy, I carefully filled in the blanks." She paused to clear her throat. "I was doing okay until I came to a box marked 'race.' There were those circles, you know, to fill in next to every choice on the list. I read down the list. It had choices like- Caucasian- African American- Latino- Asian- Native America and so on. But," she stopped and squeezed my hand. "No circle for me."

I sniffed. "What did you do?"

She looked straight at me. "I made a new circle." She said. "I colored it in and beside it I wrote 'human'."

"At my school the kids have made up this sort of club." I smiled sheepishly. "They call it the 'Freaks and Losers Club.' The cool kids pick the members by using sign language to sign a F and L behind the backs of the kids who are guilty of nothing more than being round pegs in a square peg school." I moved my fingers quickly to create the signs. "I used to laugh when I'd see the latest unsuspecting member being initiated by one of the cool kids. They would be innocently rummaging through their locker, or going into the cafeteria, or the bathroom, and then boom, quick as lightning, the sign was made. They were marked forever as a freak." I stopped and wiped my nose on my shirtsleeve. "Last year, as I turned to go into math class, I caught a group of Taylor Swift wannabes signing and laughing at me. I was devastated. You see- I hate popular music. I like Blues, and Jazz, and even that Irish stuff my mom listens to. Should that be a problem?" I questioned.

Penelope shook her head.

"I like to climb trees, swim in the slough and swing on my tire swing. And because I'm different from the others, I've been labeled a freak. A psycho."

Penelope laughed. "Well, I guess we do have something in common," she said. "We're different."

"Pretty weird. We're the same because we're different."

"Yeah," she said, standing up. "Now, tell me where to find some dish towels."

"Why?"

"Don't you think we should get the ice cream cleaned up before your parents discover it?" She pointed.

I looked at the sticky flow of chocolate ice cream that had run down the screen door and pooled into a small brown lake on the floor. I shook my head and we went to the kitchen arm and arm to get some dish towels.

And that was the end of our feud. Too bad it took the vicious mutterings of two ignorant morons to bring us together. But like my dad says, *"A good crack in our rose colored glasses is what it takes sometimes to make us take them off and see the truth more clearly."*

"Wisdom begins in wonder."

Socrates

Chapter 11

The next morning brought clear skies, and a mountain of dishes neatly stacked, and patiently waiting for someone to wash them.

"But guys," I hopelessly tried to bargain. "I'll do anything. I'll water the gardens today. What'd you say? Come on, I'm the birthday girl."

Mom stood in Dad's robe, bleary eyed. The effect from the cup of coffee she held tightly with both hands had not yet kicked in. "Well," she said blandly. "According to the calendar, you don't have another birthday for 364 days."

Dad rattled his paper. "Thanks for offering to water the gardens. You can get on that as soon as you're done with the dishes."

"This is so unfair." I stomped an angry foot.

Dad flipped his paper down. "Now listen here, young lady," he said, a touch of anger deepened his voice. "Your mom and I were up until one o' clock this morning cleaning up after a birthday party that was given for a girl who was frankly, rather sullen." I bit my lip. I wanted to tell them about what Norton and David had said, but decided it wasn't the right time.

"Fine." I said, through gritted teeth. "I'll do the dishes."

"I'll help." Penelope had appeared through the kitchen door.

Mom blinked. "Good morning, Penny," she said, giving Dad a quick glance.

"Good morning, Aunt Claire, Uncle Steve." Penelope smiled.

"Good morning." Dad sputtered.

"So," Penelope said, quickly scanning the kitchen. "Where's the dishwasher?"

"I'm standing over here next to the sink," I said sarcastically, pointing at myself.

"We have a comedian, Claire." Dad folded his paper and went to the back door.

Mom took a long final sip from the chipped green mug that she had used for coffee since I could remember. "Yeah, she's a regular Phyllis Diller," she said, adding the empty mug to the stack. "I'm going to get changed. Go on out, I'll just meet you at the barn."

"Okay," Dad said, not bothering to close the back door as he left. "It's going to be another hot one," he muttered. Heat tumbled in through the open door igniting our cool kitchen.

Penelope padded up beside me. Barefoot, she didn't seem to tower over me so very much. In fact, we were nearly the same height.

We both stared at the four large stacks of plates, serving bowls, trays and pots and pans. We looked at each other, and then Penelope asked, "Who's Phyllis Diller?"

I shrugged.

I filled our larger trough sink with hot sudsy water. We piled dishes into their bath and giggled and slapped soft bubbles, as we clinked and rinsed and dried mounds of dishes.

All the while, my parents kept nonchalantly strolling past the kitchen window throwing us quick glances. Finally, as we sopped up the last escaped suds, and hung the remaining copper stir pot, Mom burst through the back door.

"Okay, I can't stand it! What's going on between you two?"

"We're just washing dishes, Aunt Claire." Penelope stood poised.

"Yeah, Mom." I tried to stand poised too, but just looked plain clumsy. "Look, all clean and spiffy."

"No." She shook her head. This isn't right. Whatever spirits have possessed my girls, I want you to come out!"

Penelope and me looked at each other and started to snigger.

"Okay," I gave in. "You better sit down for this one, Mom."

She perched herself on the butcher block. "Spill."

So, I told her everything. I told her in detail the whole dreadful truth of how I had been jealous, and I had gone in to console myself with ice cream. I told her about the terrible words that had spilled from Norton and David's lips, but before I had gotten to the part about me and Penelope confessing our hidden truths, Mom had the phone in hand and was dialing the Frostman's residence.

The phone hadn't even warmed in Mom's angry hand before David had denied everything, and Regina had passed it off as a misunderstanding on my part and, she added, that maybe I shouldn't be sneaking around listening in on other people's private conversations.

Before Mom slammed the phone against a kitchen cabinet, she told Regina that their family was no longer welcome on our property and, she added, that cucumbers pickled in rubbing alcohol and vomit would have better flavor than the cucumbers she produced every year!

A spring from inside the demolished handset rolled against Penelope's foot. She rolled it under her toes, which were set ablaze with fire engine red nail polish. I picked up what was left of the plastic casing. "Where are you going?" I asked Mom, who had plopped off the butcher block.

"I'm going to town," she said, pulling her wallet out of her giant bag that was leaning against a kitchen chair. "I need to buy a new phone so I can call Norton's parents." She strode purposely out through the back door.

"Maybe you should buy two phones just in case you get mad again." Penelope unexpectedly called out.

Mom didn't react.

"Good one!" I snickered. "You made a joke."

Penelope smiled wide, and her eyes sparkled with her new found humor.

An idea came to me, and spread devilishly across my face.

"What?" Penelope asked, noticing my contorted features.

"Do you want to go and do something with me?"

"Depends on what you have in mind."

"I can't tell you, but trust me it'll be fun."

"Okay." She answered hesitantly. "Just promise me it will have nothing to do with Bigfoot or suspicious tire swings."

"I promise." I made a criss-cross motion across my chest.

She bit her lip before padding out the front door behind me.

"Never wrestle with pigs. You both get dirty and the pig likes it."
George Bernard Shaw

Chapter 12

"Olivia and Penelope, what a pleasant surprise!" Diane Wahl put down a basket full of aromatic herbs. The fragrance wafted gently through the air- teasing my senses. Diane's balloon of a belly sat large and pale over a long green and yellow sarong she had tied around her hips. "So what brings you two here on such a glorious morning?" she asked, adjusting the strap of the blue swimming suit top she had paired with the sarong.

"Well," I said, smiling devilishly. "We came to see your pigs!"

Penelope's eyes widened. "Pigs?"

I gave her a trusting wink.

"Well, Flopsy, Mopsy and Curly Tail haven't eaten breakfast yet." She smiled. " I think they would love to see a couple of young ladies bearing slop buckets."

"You want me to *feed* pigs?" Penelope sounded horrified.

"I'm sorry. If you'd rather just look at them, that's okay," Diane apologized. "I just thought you might think it was fun."

"No, no- I think it would be a great experience for Penelope." I leaned into Diane and whispered, "She's from the city, you know."

"Well, great!" Diane clapped her hands. "Follow me to the back porch."

The back porch was large, stretching the entire width of the back of the house. On an antique iron daybed, which was made up like a couch with a colorful crazy quilt and faded velvet brocade pillows, sat Elijah and Caleb Wahl- their lips and fingers stained red from the strawberries they were eating out of a large tangerine colored bowl.

"Hi, Libby!" Elijah said.

"Hey, Elijah, you're not a dinosaur today."

"No. I'm a dog trainer and Caleb is my dog. He's got *radies*."

"Grr!" Caleb growled. Strawberry tinted spittle ran down the sides of his mouth.

"Rabies, Elijah. He has rabies." Diane gently corrected her son. "Now, why don't you two go and wash up." She ruffled their hair as they scooted into the house. She followed them through the back door and reappeared with two 5-gallon buckets of kitchen scraps. Handing us each a bucket, we followed her through the labyrinth of flowers, trellises and oddly curving footpaths that made up the Wahl's backyard.

Flopsy, Mopsy and Curly Tail were contained under a loafing shed that was attached to the side of the Wahl's ancient barn. There was a large square cut out of the side of the barn so the pigs could escape into a stall at night, and the fence extended out and around a large alder tree- far enough for the pigs to enjoy the sun and get exercise during the day.

"Here little Piggly Wigglies!" Diane called, as three giant, pink-skinned Yorkshires stampeded through the opening in the side of the barn.

Penelope gasped, dropping her bucket and grabbing my shirt, almost knocking me to the ground.

"They're in a fence!" I said, struggling to keep standing.

"I'm sorry, but I had no idea pigs actually grew to be this size. Look at them!" She pointed. "You could ride them!"

Diane motioned for me to dump the slop buckets into their trough. "All three of my boys have ridden them at one point or another," she said to Penelope. We watched the pigs noisily devour their breakfast.

"So," Penelope said, an ill expression crossed her face. "Why do you have three enormous pigs?"

"Well, most families would butcher them," a familiar male voice interjected. "But ours aren't for eating." Jared had appeared beside his mother. His wet hair was combed back away from his face and a clean scent trailed behind him. It was the sweet scent of the verbena soap his parents made every spring.

"Mom rescued them from the mighty clutches of the volunteer firefighters raffle two years ago."

"How did you rescue them?" Penelope asked.

"I bought $200.00 worth of raffle tickets and won all three pigs, a set of knives and a milkshake from Hal's Drive-In." Diane smiled, proudly.

The pigs finished up and lumbered lazily to root out a bed under the canopy of the large alder tree.

"Do you remember the second day you were here?" I asked Penelope.

She nodded.

"You told me the only way to fit into these surroundings was to roll around in a pig pen about 50 times."

Penelope smiled sheepishly. "I did say that."

"Yes, you did!" I smiled wide.

Her eyes narrowed. "Oh, no!" she said. "You don't mean for me to get in that pen with those *creatures* and roll around fifty times?"

"No, of course not!" I said.

Relief seemed to flood Penelope's face.

"I think five times would be enough."

"I don't think so!"

Jared laughed. "Are you crazy, Livvy? I don't think you should have your cousin rolling five times in our pig pen."

Leave it to Jared to spoil my fun. Who had invited him to look at the pigs with us anyway?

But right before Penelope's smug half smile turned into a full on grin, Jared added, "She needs to roll around at least ten times to become one of us."

"I can't believe this! You're all against me." She shot Diane Wahl a pleading glance.

"I'm sorry. You're on your own. It's time for me to finish up in the herbs." She scruffled the top of Penelope's head, "You three have fun."

"So," I said. "Do you wanna go through with your countrified initiation, or are you gonna remain a city slicker for the duration of your stay?" The pigs grunted as if responding to my query.

"Okay," she gave in. "I'll do it. But only under the condition that I get to think of something creepy for you to do."

"Anything!" I enthusiastically called out. If she had asked me to roll naked in a thistle patch I would have done it. Besides, there was pretty much nothing I hadn't already done- short of eating dog poop.

Well, okay, there was that time Katie pushed me into a fresh, steaming pile Old Winder left on the side of the road, but I only got a little in my mouth and I spit it out right away.

Penelope smiled. "Are you sure the pigs won't attack me?"

"Safe as kittens." Jared said, unlatching the small gate of the enclosure. "Tell you what- I'll go in with you and keep the pigs at bay." He winked at her.

A sharp twang ran up my spine. Jealousy stroked me like an old country banjo. I shivered, trying desperately to shake off the disturbing feeling.

Penelope stood awkwardly within the confines of the pen. She pushed her toes around the dusty ground.

"Anytime you're ready!" I was having a hard time covering up the sheer pleasure I was getting from seeing Penelope in an actual pigpen. I was living out a fantasy! How many people get to do that?

"Wait a minute." Jared said. "There's something missing. Livvy, hand me a bucket."

I passed an empty slop bucket over the fence, and Jared dunked it into the pigs water trough, which was actually an old bathtub that's drain, had been corked with a whittled cottonwood branch.

He poured the full bucket onto the ground- mixing the dirt and water into a muddy bed. "There," he said, returning to the trough and rinsing his hands. "Now we have a proper pig pen for you to roll in."

I giggled.

Penelope carefully dunked a graceful foot into the thick gloppy brew. Her face brightened. "Hey, you know, it's not too bad. The consistency and cool temperature of the mud reminds me of the mud baths at a spa just south of Florence, where my mother and I spent a long weekend last spring.

"Must be nice." I commented.

"Well," Jared said. "If you think Italian mud is good, wait till you try Washington mud!"

Penelope looked at me and grinned a wide white smile. "I can't believe I'm going to do this!" Her eyes sparkled. "My parents would absolutely kill me if they saw me rolling in a pig pen wearing a $300.00 Dom Swanson." She ran a finger over the pale yellow shirt with the small red flowers embroidered around the neckline.

"Are you telling me that shirt cost $300.00?" I was shocked. "Is it spun from diamonds?"

"Olivia!" Penelope seemed offended by my fashion ignorance. "It's a Dom Swanson! You know, the famous designer known for his elegant simplicity."

"Oh, well, maybe we should trade shirts. This is a $3.00 thrift store shirt my mom just picked up for me. Something tells me that might be the safest thing to do."

"Okay, let's do this before the mud dries." Jared interrupted. "On three."

We both nodded.

"One"

Penelope sucked in her breath.

"Two."

I sucked in my breath.

"Three!"

Penelope squealed, as she dropped. The mud sucked up around her body. Coating herself completely, she looked like a corn dog before it's dropped into the fryer.

An uncontrollable giddiness seemed to possess my being. So much so, my body was seizured by fits of laughter. I leaned heavily against a fence post to keep myself standing.

Flopsy, Mopsy and Curly Tail dozed in the speckled midmorning light- barely aware of the mayhem happening within the circle of their small world. They seemed content enough with full bellies and a bed of cool soft dirt quilted with the warmth and pattern of the sun peeking through the lush green canopy overhead.

By the time Jared had counted off the tenth and final roll, I thought my sides were going to split wide open. I hadn't laughed so much since... Well, never.

"Come on, help me up." Penelope looked as helpless as a slug.

I was still giggling when I went into the pen. Jared had come too and we both grabbed a slippery arm.

"Okay," Jared said, "on three we'll pull you up."

Penelope nodded.

"One, two-"

"Augh!" Penelope, with her strange superhuman strength, I suspect from way too many strengthening exercises in ballet, pulled both Jared and me into the gloppy mud. I caught myself with my hands, splattering myself with large cool blobs of mud that ran down my face like pudding.

Jared, on the other hand, landed face first. He came up looking like some sort of mud monster from an old movie. Penelope broke out with a laughter that bubbled up from somewhere deep in the pit of her soul and exploded with volcanic propulsion. It was if she had laughed for the first time.

After the shock of having a city girl best me wore off, I started to laugh. Jared scooped up two large handfuls of mud and after slamming each of us with his muddy fast pitch, he started laughing too.

I looked at Penelope. I could tell by the glint in her eyes, we were on the same wave. Almost instantaneously, we were both slamming Jared with mud.

"Oh, my stars!" Diane Wahl's ever-patient voice ceased our play. "It looks like I've acquired three more pigs." She put her hands on her hips. "Jared, I need you to help me tie up some stakes. So as soon as you can clean up, meet me at the garden gate. You girls go ahead and enjoy your mud bath."

Oh, no, we probably should be going." I tried to sound perfectly innocent.

"Well, if you want to wash up, the hose is next to the greenhouse." She smiled.

"Thank you." Penelope squeaked between giggles.

When Diane had left, I quickly scooped up more mud and

slammed it right between Jared's eyes. "See ya, Jared!" I said, dashing for the gate. Penelope was quickly on my heels, slipping and giggling the whole way. All the while, Jared's mud bombs whistled by us, slamming fence posts and tree trunks. "Missed us!" We both said, running and giggling all the way to the hose.

The sky was a ribbon of blue lacing through the tops of giant conifers. Penelope hummed brightly behind me then started to giggle.

"What's so funny?" I asked.

"Oh, nothing." She stopped to squeeze water out her, now unrecognizable, Dom Swanson shirt. "I was just thinking about how much fun it was to wallow around in the pig pen." She twisted and squeezed at her shirt some more. Gray droplets of water hit the bumpy pavement- drying almost as soon as they hit. She giggled again.

"You did it again."

"What?"

"Laughed! What else are you thinking about?"

"Oh, not much." She grinned devilishly. "Just that this was nothing compared to what I have in store for you."

My eyes narrowed. I opened my mouth, but nothing escaped. Should I worry? I wondered. What possible stunt could she come up with that would shake me? She was bluffing, I decided. There was nothing to worry about.

That night I tucked into bed with my new journal. I smoothed my hand over the black velvet cover and traced the silver lame moon stitched with its tiny precise stitches. I opened the fragrant pages, flipping quickly to the page made with rose petals. Though it wasn't the first page in the book, it was the only flower I knew the meaning of. A rose is for love, I thought running my fingers over the bumpy page. I picked up an ink pen off my side table and awkwardly began to write:

WANDERINGS

Well, I, unlike most people have wandered to the middle of

this journal instead of starting on page one. HA!

I have started with the page laced with red roses because I remember Mama telling me that a red rose symbolizes love. I don't know what the other plants mean. Diane says to find out on my own. Maybe I will look in one of Mom's gardening books. Anyway, I guess I should write about love.

I have been learning a lot about love lately. I have learned love is the little things your parents do for you like, when my mom puts the clothes in the dryer and heats them up for me before I get dressed on cold winter mornings, or when Dad hands me the last piece of German chocolate cake, even though it's his favorite.

I've learned that sometimes love can make you feel weird and do and say stupid things. (I won't mention any names)

I've also learned that love can help you forgive someone you thought you could never forgive and that it gives you understanding and helps you see things more clearly.

And the most important love of all...well...

The words fell away as I drifted off to sleep.

"There's fennel for you, and columbines; there's rue for you; and here's some for me; we may call it herb of grace o' Sundays."
William Shakespeare

Chapter 13

"No milk." I rummaged for something to pour over my fruity "Os". "Ah Ha!" I said, pulling out the orange juice and answering our new phone at the same time. "Hey, Katie."

"How'd you know it was me?"

"Mom broke the phone yesterday yelling at Regina Frostman." I poured orange juice over two bowls of cereal and pushed one to a still groggy Penelope. "She bought a new one, it has caller ID."

"So, it is true!"

"What's true?"

"I saw Henry and Ian Walding at the grocery store yesterday. Henry said he went to visit David and he heard David's mom talking about you and your mom."

"Yeah." I answered with a full mouth of cereal. "So what did he hear?"

"Well, not much. Just a lot of – how dare that Claire Smith insult me and something about you being a little troublemaker."

"Is that all?"

"No, something like, Claire has always been jealous of my canning was mentioned too"

"I snorted. Orange juice dribbled down my chin. "Oh, Whatever!" I said, getting up to pace the kitchen floor. "First of all, her ignorant bigoted son and his equally moronic friend insulted my cousin. Mom was just reporting to Regina what had happened in hope that she would apply some good parenting skills, like, I don't know, maybe beating the daylights out of him! But no, she actually stuck up for the Neanderthal and tried to blame everything on me. That's when mom told her that her pickles would taste better if she pickled them in vomit. Then she threw the phone across the kitchen and almost chipped Penelope's toenail polish." I took a breath and Penelope gave me a thumb up as she padded to the sink with her empty cereal bowl. "So, go ahead and spread that!"

"Whoa!" Katie paused. "So, what else did you guys do yesterday?"

"Rolled around in Wahl's pig pen."

"Without inviting me? So what's going on? Are you and Penelope friends now?"

"Yeah. Pretty weird, huh."

"So, should I be jealous?"

"Give me a break, Katie! I'll call you later." I hung up the phone.

"Who would ever think orange juice would be so good over cereal." Penelope smiled. "So, what do you want to do today?"

"You're in for a special treat today, my friend." I put my arm around her.

Her smile faded.

"Don't worry- no mud, no smells, no smears. This is something pleasant." I patted her back. "I promise."

Her smile returned.

My mom stumbled into the kitchen. "You two are up early," she said between yawns. "Did you want some eggs?"

"No, thanks, Mom. We had cereal."

"How? We're out of milk."

"It's okay." I lifted the juice carton. "We used juice."

'We used juice' curiously had the same effect on Mom as coffee. "Oh, Penelope!" She said, her eyes popping open. "That is not the kind of food we usually eat. Olivia! I can't believe you fed our guest cereal with juice poured on it." Mom was now rummaging through the refrigerator. "Look," she said, pulling out an armload of food and spreading it across the kitchen table. "We have bagels and cream cheese. Look, here's some homemade jam and English muffins. We have eggs and ham. Do you want me to make you an egg McMuffin? I swear they're better than McDonalds."

"No, they're not." I whispered.

"I have potatoes. Do you want some hash browns?"

"Aunt Claire, the cereal and juice was good. I liked it. In fact I think I'll suggest it for breakfast at home sometime."

Mom sighed. She was defeated. "Well, I guess since I have all this stuff out, I'll make myself some breakfast."

"Okay, Mom, have fun. I'm going to take Penelope to the meadow. We'll be back by lunch." I kissed her warm cheek and trotted out the back door with Penelope close on my heels.

"Do not go where the path may lead, go instead where there is no path and leave a trail."

Ralph Waldo Emerson

Chapter 14

We hadn't had rain in over a month. People in Arizona or California would scoff at us for our concerns. But in Washington, a week with a nary a sprinkle is a big deal. So when we don't have any moisture for six weeks, it's a full on, four-alarm drought.

"It's breaking records!" The old guys who hang out at the gas station had been saying.

"Beryn Burg's well has already dried up. Who knows how many more are gonna go," Old Tall Tom, who always wore the same, patched jeans and hickory shirt was saying.

"It's those darn Californians!" Mr. Branson barks. "There are too many of them movin' up here with their fancy cars that cause pollution. It's getting into the air and ruining the ozone. I'm telling you, in a hundred years, this will be desert."

When I hear stuff like that I want to say, 'you know, Mr. Branson, there's more pollution leaking out of that old beater you call a vehicle than out of all the Californian cars in the area put together.' But, I don't respond. I just smile, pay for my soda and go. Everyone knows you can't argue with an old guy who hangs out at the gas station.

As I led Penelope down the trail that led to the meadow, I thought about those men. They stand in a tight circle around the new espresso machine, swearing the coffee used to taste better when it came from the old percolator. Everyday the same- same faces, same coffee, same gossip. I wondered if they were happy. What's it like to get up every morning knowing the most exciting thing in your life was going to the gas station?

Fear grasped me tightly round the neck. Oh my gosh! Would I end up like them? Is it my destiny to go nowhere and be nobody? I like it here. Would complacency become my doom? Would I become just another old person with nothing better to do than hang out at the gas station bad mouthing the tourists?

"What's wrong, Livvy?" Penelope's question shook me-bringing me back to the small worn path that wound through the apple trees and the thicket of huckleberry and oxalis and salmonberry before opening to a secret garden of sorts. A place my family calls 'The Meadow.' "You're face looks puckered. You're not going to vomit are you?"

"What's it like to be you?" I asked solemnly.

"What do you mean?"

I stopped under the knobby branches of a Jonagold and turned to Penelope. "What's it like to be able to go to Italy for a weekend? What's it like to be able to buy whatever you want? Or go to the movies anytime you want, not just when it's been a good fishing season?"

"I don't know. What's it like to have a parent waiting for you at the front door when you get home from school? Or to sit down to a *family* dinner? Just because we have a lot of money doesn't mean that my life is a dream." She sat down under the apple tree and picked the top off a dandelion. Tears flooded her eyes. "My parents just took away my best friend in the whole world and I don't feel like I can mourn my loss because everyone thinks it's stupid."

"I'm sorry." I said, sitting beside her. "Why won't they let you hang out together anymore? Did they think she was a bad influence?"

Penelope looked at me. She wiped her eyes and laughed weakly. "She wasn't a bad influence, besides, they laid her off."

"What?"

"She was my nanny. Her name is Maria Gomez and she was the best friend I've ever had." She sniffed, and then wiped her eyes again. "Maria was only 19 when they hired her to take care of me. I had just turned two. She was like a mom and big sister all rolled into one. Not only did she get my clothes ready and take me to school and all that kind of stuff, she talked to me about things. Things like boys and music. If I did well on a test, she would take me to Burger King. My parents didn't approve, so it was like our little secret. I loved sitting in the fast food restaurant talking about everyday stuff. I felt so normal. I had so much fun. You know," she said, softly. "I used to fantasize that she was my real mom." She paused. "That comment will never leave this field, right?"

"Of course not."

"Anyway, a few months ago Mom decided on a little mother-daughter weekend. She surprised me with a trip to a famous Italian spa."

"The mud bath."

Penelope shook her head. "She took me there to tell me they had decided I was too old for a nanny and that when we returned home, Maria would be gone." She threw a rock, hitting the trunk of another smaller apple tree. "I hate Italy."

"Is that who you were talking to on the phone a few weeks back?"

She smiled. "I knew you were listening in!"

I smiled sheepishly.

"Yeah, that was her. She taught me Spanish. She lives in Oregon now and is getting married next spring. I get to be the maid of honor."

I cleared my throat. "Well, I finally said, "things are usually pretty tight around here. We don't get out much. I've never been to a real play or a fancy museum. But we do rent movies and Dad makes spoon fudge. We call it that because his fudge never sets, so we eat it with spoons. We play jelly bean poker and have Yahtzee tournaments." I stood up and reached my hand down to help her up.

"I'm sorry about your friend, and I'm sorry that I assumed your life must be better because you have money. I was just having a pity party, I guess. A little worried about turning into an old guy who hangs out at the gas station. Ignore me."

Penelope's eyes narrowed. "A what?"

I laughed. "Never mind. Besides we're almost there. You're gonna love this!"

I guided her down the small path that led through the thicket. I bent the last branches back and let her go ahead of me. I wanted to see her reaction when she saw the meadow.

Penelope gasped. "This is the most beautiful place I've ever seen!"

I smiled, as we looked over a colorful crazy quilt of wildflowers spread over two acres. My great-grandmother had started the tradition. Every spring she would sprinkle large sacks of wildflower seed over the hidden field. My grandmother continued the tradition. The wildflowers have naturalized, but every year Mom and I order new wildflower seeds and sprinkle them in the field to keep up the tradition.

"I have never seen so many flowers in my entire life. There are so many colors."

Penelope was mesmerized. "This is better than a Monet."

"Mom always says, if heaven doesn't look like this, she'll be disappointed."

"I can see why."

Small puffs of cotton from surrounding cottonwood trees rode on the breeze, hanging over the field like fairy clouds. Thousands of butterflies darted from flower to flower- an insect smorgasbord of bachelor button, daisies, larkspur, poppies, lupine, for-get-me-not and columbine, a small few among the array.

"Penelope," I said. "I want to show you something. But you have to promise not to tell anyone, and most importantly. Not to laugh."

"I promise."

I couldn't believe what I was about to do. I was about to show Penelope something sacred that I had never let anyone, not even Katie or my mom, witness. I was letting her into my very own private world and even I didn't understand why. "Stay right there." I said, and I walked into the field looking back every once in awhile to make sure she was still there.

I stopped when I got to the middle of the field, closed my eyes and took a big breath. I reached my arms out, like one would who was about to fly, and I waited. I waited for the butterflies.

When I felt their soft flitting wings tickling my arms, I began to move. Slowly I twirled, weaving magic feet through the wildflowers. Dancing with butterflies. There, dancing amongst the flowers was the only place I felt graceful. There- I was beautiful. I never saw my partner as I whirled and twirled round my flowery dance floor- opening my eyes would break the spell. For if my eyes were open, I would see my knobby knees, my clumsy feet would trip, one over the other, and my coarse mop of hair would fall into my eyes.

When I opened my eyes, I half expected Penelope to be gone. But she wasn't. She was smiling softly and tears were streaking her cheeks. "Do you think I'm a psycho?" I asked.

"No," she said. "I think you're a beautiful person."

"I've been coming out here every summer since I was small to dance with the butterflies. For some reason they like me." I laughed weakly.

"There were at least a hundred butterflies covering you. It was like magic!"

"It feels like magic." I smiled. "Do you want to try?"

She reached out her hand and we laughed and skipped to the middle of the field.

"Okay," I said. "To have it work you have to be very still at first. Not until you feel the butterflies on your skin do you start to move." She looked at me intently, shaking her head to my every instruction.

That's when I heard a snap. "Listen." I looked out across the field to the forest that trimmed our property. "I thought I heard something."

Penelope put her arms back to her sides. "The branches of that tree are moving." She pointed. "And I don't think it's the wind."

"Get down." I whispered, crouching down behind pink and yellow sherbet stained snapdragons.

"What is it?" Penelope asked.

"I can't tell." I whispered. We watched as mysterious weathered hands reached out from the lower branches of a Douglas fir, bending them upward. 'Snap.' The branches broke off and a frail figure in a long woolen skirt emerged.

"Is that the old woman we met with Jared?" Penelope asked.

"Yeah," I said. "She may be very nice, but look at her." I pointed through the flowers. "I still say she's a witch."

"Whoa, a real witch. I wonder what her house looks like. Do you think she has bat ears and snake tongues in jars?"

"I don't know," I said. A wonderful idea came to me. I smiled as wide as a Cheshire cat. "How about we go and find out."

Penelope leaned in closer. "You don't mean to go to her house, do you?"

"We can run over there, poke around and be back home before she's even made it out of the woods. She's a thousand years old. She walks slow."

She smiled. "Let's do it."

"More in the garden grows, than the witch knows."
Anon

Chapter 15

We crawled as quickly as we could through the flowers and back to the edge of the thicket. We glanced back to make sure the old woman didn't see us. She was only a small form from that point- an ant in woolen wrap, busily gleaning strange treasures from the forest's edge. She hadn't noticed us.

After rambling through the thicket, we ran as quickly as we could through the apple orchard, around the garden and down our gravel drive. We stopped at the road to catch our breath.

"Are you sure you want to do this?" I said, between pants.

"Oh, I thought you weren't afraid of anything." Penelope gasped. "Lost your edge?"

I took off, with Penelope close behind, and didn't stop until we got to the small gravel road that ran along Willow Creek.

The road tunneled through the forest, with just enough sunlight breaking through the canopy to freckle the gravel with splotches of light. We jogged about a quarter of a mile, passing huge trees wrapped in jackets of green moss, and lichen hanging like Christmas garland from their giant arms. All the while, Willow Creek saturated the air with its haunting roar.

"With all this green," Penelope commented, "I feel like I'm about to enter the Emerald City."

"We're almost there," I said, pointing to a giant twisted Red Cedar. "I have only been down this road a few times in my life and this tree always creeps me out!"

"That is definitely the most unusual tree I have ever seen." Penelope said, staring up at the gnarled twisted trunk of the ancient cedar. "Like an entombed soul waiting to be set free."

" Entombed by a witch?" I asked, raising an eyebrow. I motioned for her to follow and we walked around the twisted tree, making sure to keep to the far side of the road, as not to be entrapped by whatever black magic its limbs may have held.

We followed the road across a metal bridge. The county had put it in to replace an old wood bridge that had washed out a couple of winters ago when an over abundance of rain had raised the water of Willow Creek causing it to spill its banks, flooding the surrounding forest, including Ms. Stella's property.

The road took us around a sharp bend that suddenly narrowed until it was only a footpath lined with large leathery sword ferns that tickled our legs as we brushed past. At the end of the short trail was a homemade twig fence and gate that hung on one hinge. Entwined across the top of the gate, spelled out with twisted twigs, was "Fern Cottage."

"What a cute name for a house," Penelope said, opening the crooked gate. "Fern Cott-."

"Don't say it out loud!" I put my hand in front of Penelope's mouth. "It could be a spell- a tricky way of getting rid of trespassers. You could disappear!"

"I see," she mumbled from behind my hand.

"We're going to have to act sensibly while we're here. This place could be booby-trapped with all kinds of spells. An innocent potted geranium could be enchanted to release a fragrance that could zombify you!" My old paranoia had begun to set in again. Jared's speech had become as faded and distant as a dream. This was real. She was a witch and we were going to prove it.

Once through the gate, the sky opened, revealing a small shingled cottage embellished with bits and pieces salvaged from forgotten Victorian houses. Pieces of ginger breading fastened above small paned windows. Ornate porch columns, now used to support a grape arbor, still bore their intricate painted detail- graceful reminders of a former more genteel life.

Tucked in amongst the maze of garden beds were sections of old iron fencing, a cement bird bath with moss patches, cast iron urns and antique cloches. The air sung with the tinkling of a dozen or more wind chimes that dangled from the branches of trees scattered around the property.

"This looks like something from a fairytale." Penelope said, dreamily.

"Remember to keep your wits," I warned. "In fairytales, kids are usually lured into danger by cool looking things."

We wandered down a stone path that snaked from one garden to another, finally leading us to the house. Penelope pointed to three crimson tinted geraniums perched on a small white table near the porch. We both held our breath as we tiptoed past.

The porch was cluttered with herbs and flowers planted in anything that would hold dirt: a bedpan tumbled over with creeping thyme, old work boots were planted with succulents and pails teemed with petunias. I ran my hand over the smooth, worn wooden arm of a rocking chair. It swayed gently under the pressure of my hand. The simple Dutch door that adorned the cottage, and served as the entrance, was just ever so slightly opened.

"Shall we go in?" I asked.

"That's called trespassing," Penelope pointed out. "I don't feel like spending what's left of my youth in a juvenile detention center if you know what I mean."

"We're already trespassing and besides-" I knocked the door with my foot. "Oh, look! The door is open. If anybody asks, we saw the door open and we were checking to make sure Miss Stella was okay. We didn't know she wasn't home. Besides," I put my hand on Penelope's shoulder. "Don't you want to find out if she has bat ears in jars?"

Penelope smiled. "Okay. But just a quick peek."

We stepped into the small cottage. Dried lavender and lemon balm hanging in bundles from wooden rafters perfumed the air. The wide pine planked floors gleamed, warming the room with a honey tinted glow. The kitchen and living room were combined divided only by an indigo stained worktable. On the table, scattered amongst the gardening books and small-planted plants, were bird's nests, curly twigs, feathers and smooth river stones.

An old wood cook stove squatted near a small sink that was fed by a rain catch barrel attached to the roof outside. Open shelves lined with mason jars surrounded the kitchen area. Each jar was filled and labeled.

"Do you see any jars that say bat ears on them?" I asked Penelope.

She read off the labels as she walked slowly around the kitchen. "Golden seal, chaste tree, feverfew, ginseng- I don't think there's anything but herbs up here." She shrugged. Penelope turned towards the kitchen window and froze.

"Are you okay, Penelope? Come on, keep looking. There's at least a thousand marked jars up there. Penelope?"

She looked at me. Her face was pinched and her hands trembling.

"What's wrong?" I started to panic.

"She's home." Penelope squeaked.

I scrambled to the window and looked out. Kneeling down to pet a kitten was the old woman herself.

"I'm not young enough to know everything."
J.M. Barrie,

Chapter 16

I dropped to the floor, pulling Penelope along with me. My heart played bongos in my throat, and the air around me became dry and suffocating. What was she doing here? We had run almost the whole way. We should have had plenty of time to poke around.

"She must have seen us." I said. "But I don't understand how she caught up with us."

Apparently she's faster than we thought." Penelope said, peeking out the window again. "She's taking a basket full of weeds to a shed. We have to leave now if we don't want to get caught."

We crept back out through the Dutch door to the end of the porch. I peeped around the corner of the house to make sure Ms. Stella was tucked safely in the shed. "Okay. The coast is clear," I said. "Go."

Penelope shot out, running as fast as she could across the open yard, then dropped behind the leafy skirt of a lilac tree. I followed suit, dropping beside Penelope.

"I don't think we can make it to the gate without getting caught." I said, between pants. The gate was still a good distance across the property, accessed only by trails leading through Ms.

Stella's gardens.

"What are we going to do?" Penelope sounded panicked.

I thought for a moment, then noticed our close proximity to the forests edge. "We'll cut through the woods behind us and hike to the road." I said.

"What if we get lost?"

"We won't. Remember, I've grown up here. I know how to get through the forest." I put my hand over hers.

She smiled.

I glanced around the lilac to make sure Ms. Stella was still in the shed. The door to the crooked old building with the moss coated roof was open. I could see the purple wool of her long skirt sweep past.

"She's near the door." I said. "But, I don't think she'll notice if we hurry."

We scurried into the emerald folds of the giant conifer forest that surrounded the cottage grounds. Once under it's protective canopy, we relaxed.

"Okay," Penelope's voice was calmer. "That was close. Now," she said, looking around. "How do we get out of here?"

I was leaning against a rotting stump. Red humus crumbled under my hand. I rolled it between my fingers, enjoying its cool soft fibers. "Well, I said. "There's a path." I pointed to a small worn trail. "It looks like a deer trail. We'll follow that."

"What if it leads to their lair?" Penelope seemed truly concerned.

"You mean like a hangout? Kind of like a deer biker bar?" I laughed. "Deer don't have lairs, Penelope. Come on. Follow me."

I led Penelope through the forest, over downed logs and under the tangled arms of maples. The forest was lush and hard to navigate through. The trail, clear and straight one moment, would suddenly disappear in a sea of green moss and thick branches, only to reappear six or seven feet from where it should have been. I tried to act perfectly confident, but if the truth were known, I had never been in that part of the forest before and I was afraid I was getting us lost.

The only thing I did know to do was to follow the creek. I used the constant sound of water rushing over rock as a guide. I would get us to Willow Creek. Willow Creek led to the road. But wait a minute. I stopped in the middle of the trail. A shiver ran down my spine.

"What's wrong?" Penelope cried out. "Are we lost?"

"No," I turned toward her. "I was just thinking. We had to cross the creek to get to Ms. Stella's."

"Yeah."

"That means we'll have to cross it again to get back to the road."

"So."

"So, there's no bridge to cross the creek out here."

Penelope's mouth dropped. "Oh," she finally said. "What are we going to do?"

"I guess we'll wade through the creek." I said stupidly. What was I thinking? I had almost killed myself trying to get through Willow Creek once before. But, I reassured myself, I was thirteen now, I was stronger and more physically and mentally capable of crossing the creek.

"Are you sure we can handle the current?" Penelope asked. That creek seemed kind of swift."

"Penelope," I said, haughtily. "Do you really think that I would take us across the creek if I didn't think it was safe."

She looked square into my eyes. "Yes. Yes, I do."

"We'll be fine. Come on." I motioned for her to follow.

We stumbled through thimbleberry bushes and around devil's club. We tripped over roots and ferns, until finally we were at the creek's edge.

A cool wet mist rose above the frothy folds of Willow Creek. Droplets formed on our arms and faces- a refreshing release from the heat that penetrated the forest's canopy.

"You have got to be kidding me." Penelope said. "There is no way we can cross that!" She pointed stiffly at the angry water that noisily slapped the large mossy boulders that littered its bed.

"Well," I scratched my head. "As I see it, we have three options. We can try to cross the creek here. As you can see," I pointed across the creek, "that twisted old cedar tree we walked past earlier, is right over there. We can then walk safely down the gravel drive to Apple Road. Another option would be to try and follow the creek to Apple Road from this side of the creek. Unfortunately, I'm not very familiar with this part of the forest. This creek could rise and fall and wind all over the place before leading us back to the road. We might not make it out until nightfall, and that means we would really get into trouble. Our third option is to go back to Ms. Stella's and try to sneak out through the gardens and cross the bridge there." I sighed heavily. "It's up to you."

Penelope threw her hands into the air. "So much for knowing your way through the forest. *I've grown up here.*" She mimicked my voice. *"I know where I'm going."*

I rolled my eyes.

"Oh, what the heck." She laughed, nervously. "Let's cross the creek. I might as well. I've eaten dinner from a stick; I've had conversations with strange people who appear out of the woods with wheelbarrows; I've rolled in a pig pen along side three monster sized pigs, and I've broken into a lady's home in search of bat wings. I might as well go ahead and cross this *stupid* creek."

Whoops. I had screwed up. She was ticked at me. "I'm sorry." I weakly tried to apologize.

"No. It's okay." She stopped. The corners of her mouth turned up. "This is the most fun I've had in my life. Pretty pathetic, huh?"

"Still," I continued. "It was my idea to sneak to Ms. Stella's house. I fear I've got us in quite a fix, and if we don't get through this without getting into very big trouble, I promise I'll make sure everybody knows it was my fault."

"I have free will, Olivia." Penelope chortled. "If I didn't want to go, I would have told you so. Now," she slapped me on the back. "Let's get across this stupid creek and get back to the house. I'm starving."

We picked a spot on the creek that we felt would be easiest to cross. Penelope stepped into the creek first. I followed, hanging tightly onto the back of her shirt. If she fell, I wanted to be able to keep her from going down stream.

Penelope gasped as her feet plunged into the icy water. I held my breath as, I too, drove my feet into its frigid folds. Shocks of cold seemed to paralyze my limbs. It had all come back- the strength of rushing water. I instantly felt out of control, and I could tell by the look on Penelope's face, she was faring no better.

"I'm going to try to take a step!" Penelope called over the roar of the water.

I shook my head and grasped her shirt tighter.

She lifted her foot, but instantly started to lose her balance. As her body collapsed into the icy water, my hands, numb from the cold, lost hold of her shirt. I watched in horror as my cousin was washed down stream, finally, slamming against a large boulder some 20 feet from where I was.

"Penelope!" I screamed. "Hang on to the rock! I'll come get-" Before I had finished my sentence, I too, was swept away. I felt like I was in a washing machine- churning and rolling until- BAM! I hit something hard. I raised my head, coughing and gasping for air.

I had been washed against the same boulder Penelope was grasping onto. Her eyes were glazed with an icing of fear and she was trembling uncontrollably. "What now?" Her voice shook.

I looked to the bank for answers. We were so close. If only I had something to grab onto, I thought, I could pull us out. I reached for a willow sapling that gracefully curved over the creek. My fingertips grazed its soft leaves, but it was no use. I couldn't grasp it.

"Don't you know enough to not go near water that screams? Grab on." It was the old woman. Her face was a twisted scowl, as she extended a long carved staff towards us.

I didn't know which I was more afraid of, her or the water. I desperately took hold of the staff. She pulled, guiding me safely to the bank.

Then it was Penelope's turn. "I'm afraid!" She yelled. "Ah, come now, child, grabbing hold of a stick is but the simplest of trials."

She reluctantly grabbed the staff and her body trembled as she was guided to the lush creek bank.

Ms. Stella took off her apron and handed it to Penelope. "There you go, Miss Penelope. Dry off as best you can."

"Thank you," Penelope squeaked.

Directing her attention to me, the old woman said, "This is the second time I've pulled you from the water. I'm not getting any younger and I may not be able to save you a third time." She chuckled.

I didn't care to reply to my rescuer. Instead, I nuzzled deeper into the soft moss, letting the dappled sunlight that splashed upon me penetrate my skin, warming me from the inside out.

Penelope finished with the apron and tossed it to me. I patted my face and arms. The apron smelled like Ms. Stella's house- lavender and lemon balm.

"Come on, girls." She motioned for us to get up. "I think you two need a nice cup of tea," she said, picking up her basket.

We silently followed her down a well-worn path that lie slightly east of the hullabaloo of vegetation I had tried to navigate us through.

Ms. Stella's basket spilled over with the delicate tendrils of some small leafy plant. I wondered if they were for eating or for spells.

"Nasturtum officinale." She said. "Watercress- slightly peppery. A very good potherb. I get it from the pool that's not to far from here. That's where I was when I heard your cries." She stopped and looked at me with narrowed eyes. "Pools whisper. It's okay to splash about in water that whispers."

Okay, I was officially freaked out. She was a mind reader. I spent the rest of the walk trying desperately to keep my mind free of thought.

"Count your age by friends, not years. Count your life by smiles, not tears."
John Lennon

Chapter 17

The cottage ground opened before us- a candy land of color and light. We stepped through allowing the full energy of the sun to warm our bodies.

She led us to what she called her *summer kitchen*. It lay on the south side of the property, tucked behind a hedge of wild dog roses.

It was a small screened house that was furnished simply with a small wood cook stove, a long pine table, stacked with canisters, a few books and boxes underneath. Pots hung from a makeshift pot rack of driftwood. A rocking chair sat lonely in one corner, and a cot, piled with folded blankets and pillows, in another.

"There used to be two cabins on this property. Ms. Stella explained. "This being the smaller of the two. It was in pretty bad shape, so I hired a carpenter to take out the walls and replace supports where needed. He patched the roof and replaced the exterior walls with screen. I think the poor young man thought I was a bit senile-wanting him to build me a screen house. But-" she paused, smiling. "There is nothing more beautiful than sitting out here on warm evenings with a soothing cup of tea and watching what nature has to offer up as entertainment. Some nights it's a chorus of bullfrogs.

Other nights, I'm tickled by the antics of a family of raccoons. And my favorite nights, when I am truly honored with the serene beauty of true silence."

She stopped and filled a kettle with water from a water jug she kept on the long table. "Better than television." She said, putting the kettle on the wood cook stove that was already fired up.

I still hadn't said anything. Being there reminded me of the story of Hansel and Gretel. I was getting nervous with her spending so much time by the wood cook stove. As she chatted, my mind began to hum with uncertainty. *Was she a witch? Was she reading my mind right at that moment? Did she know the agony I was going through? Maybe she was trying to scare us. Maybe the added adrenaline flavored our flesh. Was she going to eat us tonight, or make us into jerky and save us for the winter?* I was going crazy.

"If you're gonna eat us, just do it now!" leapt uncontrollably from my mouth. She stopped talking, and gazed at me with a peculiar squinted expression.

Penelope covered her face with her hands and moaned. I know she was as scared as I was. I think she thought I had made things worse.

We all just stood there for what felt like an eternity, like soft fleshy statues, until finally, Ms. Stella started to chuckle. I was waiting for her to transform into a hideous she-beast. But she didn't. Her chuckling turned to laughter. She slapped her leg.

"Oh, child, is that why you thought I brought you here?" She wiped her watery eyes. "I suppose you think my tongue was cut out by a rejected lover too, huh?" She laughed some more and stuck her tongue out for us to see.

"So, you're not a witch?" Penelope asked.

"Heavens, no!" Ms. Stella answered, holding back another chuckle. "But don't go telling everybody. I like a bit of mystery." She winked.

"But-" I finally choked out. "Back there, in the woods, you read my mind."

"What?"

"I was wondering what was in your basket. You answered."

"I was just trying to make conversation. I didn't know you

were thinking about my treasure, and I didn't mean to frighten you." She smiled coyly. "Besides, shouldn't it be I who is frightened by you girls." She turned to take the teapot off the stove.

Penelope looked at me. I shrugged my shoulders.

"I believe breaking and entering is a crime." Ms. Stella said, softly.

I gasped.

"We didn't mean any harm. We just wanted to see if you had any-" Penelope's words trailed off.

"You were looking for the evidence." Ms. Stella said and pulled a quart jar from a box. "You wanted to prove I was a witch." She pulled two plastic bags from another box. They were full of what looked to be dried crumpled leaves. "Chamomile and Peppermint," she said, packing the empty quart jar with the dried herbs. She then took the kettle and poured the hot water over the herbs filling the jar to the brim. "Well, we have a couple of minutes," she said, screwing a lid onto the jar. "Tea needs to steep. Shall we take a walk through the gardens?"

"This phlox," she boasted. "Was just a small shoot when I transplanted her here just last spring." Look at her, such a big girl now. You'd think she'd been planted here for centuries. So big. So lush. And look at those buds." She smiled. "I believe great things are in this flower's future."

Penelope snorted.

"You find me amusing?"

"Well," Penelope pointed out, "It does seem that maybe you spend too much time in your garden."

I was surprised by Penelope's boldness.

Ms. Stella looked keenly at Penelope. "Do you really think so?"

"Well," Penelope answered cautiously, "Yeah- I suppose I do. You're talking about that flower like it's *alive*."

"Ah! But it is alive."

"I know *that*." Penelope was flustered. "I mean alive, as in a living person, alive. You called it a *her*- like it was your daughter."

Ms. Stella put her hand on Penelope's shoulder. "My dear, Ms. Penelope, these are my children."

"But they can't talk to you or play or anything."

"You'd be surprised. Flowers and herbs have a language all their own." She gave Penelope a squeeze. "Follow me."
I stood back watching the two of them walking together- the old woman and the girl laughing, arm and arm, as they strolled through the sun-dappled gardens. Penelope had accepted her. She had embraced her strange ways. I would have never expected that from her. But, as she's been teaching me, sometimes you need to give people a chance.

Ms. Stella turned back. "Come on, Olivia. I want to show this to you, too."

I waved.

Ms. Stella had accepted me too. She had accepted me even though I broke into her house, made jokes about her behind her back and made her risk her life to rescue me, not once, but twice. And what thanks did I ever give her? None. Did she see something in me that I had not yet discovered? She was unlike any other person I had ever known.

"Look," she said, pointing to a bumblebee as it flashed by.

"Look at what?" Penelope asked.

"You missed it," I said. "But don't worry it was just a really big bug. It would have freaked you out."

Penelope shivered.

"It was a bumblebee," Ms. Stella said. She shook her finger playfully at me. "Don't you dare refer to him as just a *bug*. The bumblebee is regarded as royalty round these parts."

I sniggered.

"You see, girls," Ms. Stella said, as she walked. "If you slow down and watch nature it will let you in on its secrets." She stopped and inhaled- taking the sweet air deep into her lungs. "Just think," she spread out her arm. "All this beauty, color and scent evolved to lure pollinators. Look at my darling child here." She cupped her hands around a pink bloom.

"Foxglove." I said.

"Why, yes, Olivia!" She seemed surprised. "Or, as this beauty here prefers, Ms. Digitalis. She has special markings- see" She lifted one of its trumpeted blooms. "A speckled throat. Helps those pollinators zero in on their sugary target."

"So," Penelope asked. "How do the flowers talk to you?"

"Ahh!" Ms. Stella said. We followed her to a yellow rose bush. She snipped off two long stems and handed one to each of us. "There." She said.

"I don't understand." Penelope leaned over and smelled the rose.

"Well," Ms. Stella explained. "A long time ago, people used flowers to send messages. I gave each of you a yellow rose which signifies friendship."

Penelope flashed a smile. "That is so cool!"

"So," I tried to sound nonchalant. "What if I gave you a few sprigs of, I don't know, maybe, lemon balm?"

"Herbs just happen to be my specialty." She motioned for us to follow.

We followed her to a large circular garden that was enclosed by a split rail cedar fence. "This is my favorite garden," she said, opening the rustic bent willow gate. The garden greeted us with butterflies and bees wafting on an aromatic breeze. It was separated by intersecting paths that carved the garden into four pie-shaped beds, which were labeled with wooden garden stakes. We walked to the section labeled 'tea,' and there amongst the bee balm, chamomile, costmary and mints, were several bright green lemon balm plants. Ms. Stella snapped off several sprigs- releasing the citrus fragrance.

"Here," she said, presenting me with the sprigs. "Melissa Officinalis. A wonderful nerve relaxant and antioxidant."

I wrinkled my nose as I took the offering. I was confused. Was the reason Diane Wahl had laced pages of my journal with lemon balm because she thought I needed to relax? How rude.

"But," Ms. Stella continued. "In the language of flowers an offering of lemon balm is for pleasant memories."

I smiled. "How about lavender?"

Ms. Stella smiled. "For luck."

"And thyme?"

"Courage."

"Feverfew?"

"Protection." She gently brushed the herbs as walked through them. Their scents rose, mixing on the breeze and teasing our nostrils.

"What about sage?"

She stopped. Then turned and looked at me quietly. "Wisdom." She continued to walk back towards the cottage. We followed. "The wisdom to use this one life you are given in a useful way," she continued. "To waste one's life is a tragedy. Be happy. Make good choices and live your life to the fullest."

Back at the summer kitchen Ms. Stella finished preparing our tea and brought it to us in delicate china teacups.

"My grandmother's china," she commented.

"It's beautiful." Penelope said.

The tea was hot, and slightly sweet from the fireweed honey she had laced it with. We sat quietly sipping tea and listening to a starling serenade. Time stood still here. I didn't feel the need to hurry. I only needed to relax and enjoy good company and good tea.

As I sipped, bubbles floated to the surface of my cup, tickling my lips. "Ah," Ms. Stella commented. "According to folklore, that is a sign that you will soon be receiving a kiss."

"I don't think so, I said. I could feel my face heat up as the image of Jared flashed before me.

"She's blushing!" Penelope said, and she and Ms. Stella giggled.

Ms. Stella excused herself and when she returned she had made two beautiful bouquets of big Shasta daisies, yellow roses, lavender, yarrow, thyme and sage sprigs- then handed one to each of us.

"Yellow roses for friendship," she said, pointing to the flowers. "Yarrow for good health, thyme for courage, lavender for luck, daisies for simplicity and sage for wisdom. You may want to hang a few sprigs of the sage over your beds at night." She chuckled. "Be careful. No more crossing noisy water. Understand me?"

"Yes," we both said.

She gave us both tight hugs before we left. "Olivia, she said before I walked into the garden. "I'm glad to see you have such an interest in herbs."

"Well," I had to be honest. "I didn't until a few nights ago when Diane Wahl gave me a journal. She made the paper herself and put different herbs in them. She told me each page had a meaning and that it was up to me to find out what they mean."

"I know Diane, Well. I know how fond she is of you." She patted my head. "That sounds like a pretty special journal. Enjoy."

"I will."

I ran to catch up with Penelope and we both waved before pushing through the little gate with the twisted twig letters that spelled out 'Fern Cottage.'

We walked silently back home, each contemplating, in our own way, the morning we had just experienced.

I felt a shift at that time- a movement of heart or soul. I don't really know how to express it, but I do know I felt different. Wiser. Had the bouquet she gave me made the change? I brought it to my face. The rose petals were like silk upon my cheek. And the scent was of a clear summer morning. But, at the same time, I felt sad. I had realized at that very moment that I had denied myself a friendship because of what I had feared. I vowed, right there, not to let fear or jealousy get in my way again.

"As Rosemary is to the Spirit, so Lavender is to the Soul."
Anonymous

Chapter 18

Later that evening, I sat on my crumpled bed and flipped through my moon journal. I moved my hand over each bumpy page remembering their meanings. Thyme for courage, lemon balm for pleasant memories, lavender for luck, red rose petals for love, feverfew for protection and sage for wisdom.

"Livvy!" my mom's voice startled me.

"Yeah, Mom." I called back.

"I need to see you."

"Coming!" I said, then put my journal away, jumped off my bed, hopped over my three piles of clothes and tumbled out the door.

I was startled to see Mom and Penelope right outside the door. Mom had Dad's robe over her arm and Penelope had some fancy bottle of French shampoo.

"What's going on here?" I questioned.

"It's time." Penelope smiled wide.

"Wait a minute." I slipped my mom a pleading glance. "I don't know what you're talking about. It looks to me like you're going to *try* to get me in a bathtub or something."

"Remember when you told me if I rolled in the pig pen that

you'd do something creepy for me?"

"But a bath? When I made that agreement, I thought you meant something fun."

"Like rolling in a *pig-pen*?" Mom asked, sarcastically.

"Yeah!" I answered. "This isn't fair. Nobody said anything about bathing. Especially with *frou-frou* soap." I pointed stiffly at the fancy glass bottle.

"Oh, this isn't just a bath with *frou-frou* soap." Penelope said. "This is a makeover!"

The words ricocheted off my eardrums and exploded in my brain. Makeover! I was living a nightmare! "Mama?" I gave her my best puppy face "Aren't you going to stop her?"

"No!" she said. "I'm going to help her."

"Yeah," Penelope said. "You're mom's going to guard the door to make sure you don't try to escape. Oh, by the way, don't even think about trying to sneak out the window. Your dad's outside and said, if forced, he would drag you back here kicking and screaming." She punctuated her sentence with a satisfied, "Hmpf."

"Here." My mom tried to hand me the robe.

"No." I said, desperately. "I can't do this."

"I'll be in my room getting the makeup ready!" Penelope chuckled. "Oh, by the way, she said, handing me the shampoo. "This shampoo will leave your hair shiny and soft feeling without the heavy residue some shampoos can leave behind. Use it." She giggled. "Isn't this going to be fun?"

I watched numbly as Penelope chuckled all the way to her room. I had wondered what she could come up with that could be worse than eating dog poop. Well, she figured it out. I couldn't believe her. A bath in the middle of the week and makeup too? It was so unfair. It was evil. I searched my mom's eyes for some scant sign of sympathy. Nothing. Her eyes were as dead as the robin corpse I scraped off the sidewalk a few days before.

She pointed to the bathroom. I jerked the robe off her arm and went in.

The tub was already filled. Soft, foamy bubbles spilled over the sides of the tub. Candles were lit and the whole room smelled of Jasmine. I peeled off my t-shirt and shorts and slipped slowly into warm, scented water. Ever so carefully, I slid down into the tub, until only my head was sticking out. I felt every muscle in my body relax. And as much as I tried to hate it, it was- dare I say…Nice. You could have hung me from my ears and jabbed bamboo skewers under my fingernails. I would've never admitted to the comfort I felt in that tub filled with fancy smelling soap and lit by candlelight. I was miserably under its spell.

I washed my hair with the French shampoo, dried off with a fluffy towel, wrapped myself in my dad's huge robe and padded out into the hall.

Mom was still standing there with a big goofy grin on her face. "Be a good sport." She said, as I walked past. I rolled my eyes.

I hadn't been in our spare room since Penelope's arrival. It was kind of a hobby room, storage room and guest room all in one. Penelope had done her best to make it her own. Next to an abandoned easel and several boxes of Christmas decorations, she had neatly stacked her suitcases. Placed on the makeshift bedside stand (it was really an old TV tray) was a novel, 'Of Mice and Men' (We had rented the movie once and it was completely depressing), a travel alarm, a roll of peppermint lifesavers, and a bottle of Purell instant hand sanitizer. She had even gone as far as to hang a poster of some ballet dancer above the twin size wagon wheel bed we had provided for her comfort. It was actually my dad's- a remnant from his youth, complete with flannel cowboy sheets and blue and red plaid comforter.

Penelope stood in front of a card table she had set up with about a million different tubes and bottles. There were so many beauty supplies, I would have sworn the make-up counter of C and D drug and Sundries had moved into our spare room.

"What are you staring at?" I questioned my grinning cousin.

"I don't know. I've never seen you this clean before." She snorted.

"Okay, very funny. Well, let's get this over with." She sat me down on a stool and jerked my shoulders.

"Ouch!"

"You need to sit up straight," she said.

The towel was whipped off my head and my hair plopped down like a wet mop covering my face.

"I'm definitely going to need the detangler," she said, reaching for a purple bottle and a wide toothed comb. "I hope I have enough. You have the thickest hair I've ever seen." I coughed and sputtered as she saturated my head with the sweet smelling detangler.

"Oh, stop being such a baby." She laughed. "I thought you weren't bothered by anything," she said, jerking the comb through my hair, snapping my head back.

"I'm not bothered by anything unless it includes a great amount of pain. This is killing me!" My head was jerked back again, as she tugged at my heavy hair. I can't believe people go to salons and have this done on purpose." Another tug. I grimaced. My head snapped back.

As she combed, Penelope started to hum. Her humming, soft at first, became louder, keeping time with the tugging of my hair. She was enjoying herself. "You know," I said, "I'm totally suffering here. You could at least pretend to be sympathetic."

"I can't help it," she said. "This is a dream come true. I always knew you needed a good makeover. I just never imagined, not even in my craziest dreams, that I would be the one performing the *magic*." She punctuated her comment with a smooth wave of her comb through the air.

"It's going to take a lot more than a wave of a comb to make me beautiful."

She lifted the hair away from my eyes. "Now what kind of comment is that?"

"Be real, Penelope, I'll never be as pretty as you. You have beautiful dark skin and shiny black hair. Your teeth are straight and white." I sighed. "Let's face it, were opposites in *every* way."

She looked quietly at me.

"You know, Penelope," I said, remembering her phone conversation with Maria. "I was never ashamed of you because you're black. I pushed you away and played mean tricks on you because I was jealous. I justified my actions by thinking you deserved it because I thought you were a spoiled brat. But in hindsight, I think I did it because being around you made me feel, I don't know, small. You are beautiful and rich. The world is yours. I'm poor and plain." I let out a long slow breath. "There. I said it. I hope you'll still be my friend."

"Oh." Her combing became softer. "I was pretty mean to you when I first came here too." She laughed. "I called you some pretty mean names. I'll admit this was the *last* place I wanted to be. I felt like my parents dumped me- and I was trying to punish you for it." She was silent for a moment. "I'm glad you told me what you did about the color of my skin. I'm proud of my heritage. It makes me feel special. But you're right. I did think you were embarrassed that I was your cousin and it made me angry. So, sometimes, I would try to make you jealous by showing off my family's material assets. I don't think I made a very good first impression with your friends either. I made a complete idiot of myself on that little walk with your friend Jared." She lifted my chin. "But everything changed the night of your birthday. What you did for me that night was probably the coolest thing anybody has ever done. It took a lot of guts to stick up for me like that. Believe me, Olivia- you are not small."

I smiled.

The comb was sliding easily through my hair now, but my scalp felt like it was on fire.

"Ahh," Penelope said. "This is more like it. Time to blow dry."

The dryer roared as it blew its hot breath onto my sore scalp. Penelope stopped only once to squeeze some goop out of a long white and pink tube, smoothing it onto my hair before blasting my head with more heat.

When she was done, my head felt lighter than it had ever felt. I didn't have a mirror, but what I could see was smooth and glistened under our 60-watt bulbs.

Penelope's eyes lit up. "Time for makeup!"

I sucked in my breath. The only time I had ever worn makeup was for a Christmas concert last winter. I had had a sleigh bell solo for our sixth grade rendition of 'Jingle Bells.' Mom had insisted on a touch of lipstick and mascara, as well as a really stupid looking pink dress with big puffy sleeves. Why is it when you're already under pressure, parents like to make you feel even more uncomfortable by making you look like an idiot?

Penelope picked up a few shades of lipstick and held them up to my face. "Hmm," she said. "Though you're blonde and extremely fair, you seem to have bluish undertones." She marked my hand with a shimmering pink tube. "Yes, I most definitely would say you're a winter.

"Oh, just slap some make-up on me and get it over with." I sighed and slumped forward.

"Olivia, it's important." She pulled my chin up. "Please, just cooperate."

"Fine."

I patiently sat through the powder, and liner and mascara nightmare. As well as putting up with lipstick and blush, I also endured glossing and polishing. I felt like one of those Barbie heads you buy little girls. You know how the head just sits there with a stupid grin on its face, helpless against the little twerp, who's plastering it with whatever makeup they chose (including markers or ink pens). When would the agony end?

Penelope stood back-poised with her hands on her hips. She cocked her head. She smiled wide. "I think I created a masterpiece," she said.

"Well," I said, glancing around the room. "Where's the mirror. Let me look so I can go wash my face."

"Wait." Penelope walked over to her bed. Across it lie a creamy gauze dress covered in tiny blue violets. "Happy Birthday," she said, holding the dress up.

"For me?"

"Yeah. I didn't give it to you on your birthday." She looked coyly to the floor. "It's a Dom Swanson."

"Known for his elegant simplicity?"

"Yeah." She smiled. "Look, I'm going to go and get your parents. While I'm gone, I want you to put this on. The leather sandals go with it." She pointed to a pair of flat brown sandals sitting on the bed." She put the dress back on the bed and left the room.

I walked over to the delicate garment and pressed the fine material between my fingers. I hadn't put on a dress since the Christmas concert. I was nervous. I slipped off my dad's robe. The dress felt good sliding on. It was form fitting, but not tight to my hips- it hung airily almost to my ankles. It was as comfortable as one of my dad's t-shirts, but much more…elegant. The sandals fit too. I walked

119

around the room. No squeaks.

I felt weird.

Penelope knocked lightly on the door. "Are you ready?" She asked.

"As ready as I'll ever be. Come on in."

Penelope pushed the door open. She and my parents stood huddled under the jamb with jaws dropped around their feet.

"Well," I said, feeling uncomfortable under the three sets of unblinking eyes. Do I look as stupid as I feel?"

My mom started sobbing. Not little feminine snuffles, like the kind you hear in the movie theater when someone is trying desperately to hold their composure when a character dies. No- my mom was sobbing uncontrollably. The kind of sobbing that includes loud blubbering noises and mucus. She came up to me quickly, gathering me in her arms. "You're so grown up. I can't believe this beautiful young woman is the same little girl who was scraping a dead bird off the sidewalk for me just two days ago."

"Mom, you're squishing me." I coughed.

"Honey, you look like a super model." My dad said. "I better get my shotgun cleaned up, Claire. It looks like I'm going to be chasing off the boys."

"Dad." I rolled my eyes.

"Well." Penelope asked, "are you ready to see yourself?"

"Yeah, let's get this over with." I said.

She walked over to the closet where a full-length mirror hung on the inside of the door. "Okay." She said, after opening the door. "Take a look."

I stepped silently in front of the door. Was this a trick mirror? I wondered. Because reflected before me was not a scrawny, shaggy headed, clumsy girl- but a tall, willowy young woman, with shiny golden hair that hung neatly past her shoulders, soft gray eyes and a perfect pink mouth. That stranger in the gauze dress was beautiful. She was me.

Penelope came up behind me and said in my ear, "Plain, *you* are not."

I smiled and turned to my glowing family. "Not too shabby." I said.

They all laughed.

A slight rapping sound climbed the stairs and echoed through Penelope's room.

"Is there someone at the door?" I asked.

"I don't know." Mom said. "Did you hear something?"

The sound rose again- this time louder.

"There it is again," I said. "There is definitely someone knocking at the door."

"Why don't you go and answer it, Livvy," my dad said, casually.

"I can't." I said. "I gotta change."

"You were asked to answer the door, Sweetie," my mom said.

"Why should I answer it?" I questioned. "I'm all gooey with makeup." I was becoming annoyed. It would have been a lot easier for one of my parents to hop down the stairs. They were wearing sweat pants, for crying out loud I was wearing a dress and new shoes.

"Mind your father and go answer the door!" My mom's voice rose and she pointed stiffly toward the hall.

Penelope put her arm around my shoulder. "Take my advice," she said, sweetly. "Just go answer the door. Who knows, you might be happy you did."

'*You might be happy you did*' What was that supposed to mean? I stomped down the stairs. By that time, our visitor was rapping with more force. "I'm coming!" I yelled. "If you break our door," I yelled, as I swung it open. "You're gonna have to pay for..." Oh my gosh! It was Jared. "It." I squeaked.

He was as speechless as I was. He just stared at me with his mouth open. "Livvy?" He finally questioned. "Is that you?"

"Penelope gave me a bath," I stammered.

His eyes narrowed.

I shook my head. "I mean- I gave myself the bath. Penelope did the rest." I looked sheepishly to the ground.

"You look so different," he said.

I smiled at him. "You think so?"

"Yeah! You look pretty. You know, you look like a girl."

This time my eyes narrowed.

"I didn't mean it like that." He shook his head. "I mean you look really nice, Olivia."

"Really?"

"Really." His face turned red.

I was floating. *I* made Jared blush. Me! Me! Me! I felt empowered. I felt like a woman! What womanly gesture would I do next to convey my approval of his actions? "You don't mean it," I said and punched him in the arm. He flinched.

"Of course, I do." He smiled, and rubbed his arm. "Oh, before I forget, your cousin had called. She said you needed to borrow our atlas. He bent around and picked up the book he had set down on the porch. "Here."

Suddenly, it had all become very clear. '*You might be happy you did*' flashed vividly in my brain. I had been setup. I took the book and turned to place it in the house. I looked up. There they were, all three of them, grinning at me from the top of the staircase. My parents gave me a thumbs up sign before tiptoeing to their room.

"Well," Jared said. "Maybe, if you want, we could take another walk sometime. You know, after your cousin goes home."

Maybe it was because I was stirred by Jared's gesture, or maybe it was because I had been holding my breath and the lack of oxygen was affecting me, but I actually fell right there on the porch. Yes, right there, in front of Jared, I dropped to my knees. As I fell, I tried to catch myself by grabbing the wall. Instead, I ended up smacking the backside of my hand and dropped anyway.

"Are you okay?" He asked, as he guided be back to a standing position.

"I'm fine." I said, humiliated. "I just knocked my knuckles against the side of the house when I fell. No big deal" I rubbed my sore hand. "It's the new shoes. I guess I'm not used to them."

"Let me see your hand," he said. He took my hand in his. "Oh, you might want to use an ice pack," he said. 'It will stop the swelling."

"Thanks." I stammered.

He smiled at me. Then he did something I will never forget for the rest of my life. He gave my knuckles a little rub then he kissed my hand. Okay, it was more of a gentle peck. But, his lips did touch my skin.

"I think you'll live," he said. "Take two aspirin and call me in the morning."

I smiled, but didn't speak.

"Well," he said, returning my hand. "I'll see you around, Livvy."

"Bye," I said. I watched him bound down the porch stairs and disappear into the moonless night. He had enchanted me. I felt as though I was floating. I never wanted the feeling to end.

"Oh, my gosh!" Penelope's squealing broke the spell. "I can't believe it. He kissed you." She was jumping up and down. "Are you excited? I can't stand it. How did it feel?"

"Well," I said, still a bit dazed. "I don't think that really qualified as a kiss. He just kind of brushed my knuckle with his lips." I giggled. "It was kind of like a million butterflies touching my hand." I took a breath. "I can't believe you set me up."

"I could tell there was something going on." Penelope sniggered. "Every time you're around him you turn into a blubbering fool. And," she added, "he's not much better."

"What?" I couldn't believe she had said that. "He doesn't even know I'm alive."

"Oh, he knows, my friend." She patted my shoulder. She was quiet for a moment. "You know what's weird about this?" She said.

"What?"

"Ms. Stella predicted it."

I thought for a moment. "The bubbling tea! Oh, my gosh, maybe she is a…"

Penelope was shaking her head. "No, she's not a witch."

"You're right." I felt ashamed for having the thought.

"I'll tell you what she is, Livvy."

"What?"

"She's a Sage."

"I don't understand."

"That's what my mom calls people who are very wise. A Sage."

It made sense. Since sage was a symbol for wisdom. I smiled. "Yeah. I like that. You know, she was very cool. She wasn't stressed about anything, and she had a lot to be stressed about if you think about it. No electricity, No running water-"

"No flushing toilet." Penelope added.

"I guess life is what you make of it."

"Goodnight, cousin. It's been a long day."

"Thank you, Penelope."

"You're welcome. The dress looks like it was made for you."

"No, not for the dress, which I do love, by the way," I said, pressing the filmy material between my fingers. "I wanted to thank you for coming here this summer. Thank you for accepting me. I've had a lot of fun."

Penelope gave me a tight hug. "Isn't it funny how things work out sometimes." She pulled back. "In a matter of a few short weeks, our lives have changed so much." She smiled. "Goodnight, Livvy," she said, and went back into the house.

I was left alone. The night was completely still except for the moths that bumped over and over against our porch light. I watched them as I reflected on Penelope's last sentences. Life *was* funny, I had decided. A few weeks before, if someone had told me I would be standing there that very night- having just been kissed by Jared and wearing a dress and makeup, I would have punched them.

The moths were still bumping, like fluttering crazy balls- boing-boing-boing off our porch light. Every once in a while one would get trapped in the opaque shade and I watched their small shadows struggle until they fell lifeless, pooling with other bug remains. I needed to remind someone to clean that shade out, I thought as I lazily tromped back up the stairs to my room.

Cozied up in my bed, dress and makeup free, I opened my moon journal to the page laced with lavender (for luck). I wrote with my best handwriting:

How lucky I am to have made a new friend today. Ms. Stella is a fine woman. I look forward to many more quiet moments with her- sipping tea and listening to the bird song.

And how lucky I am because today Jared...

I'm almost afraid to write it down- I'm afraid the experience will leak out of my pen and it will have never happened...

I have decided not to write the words, but I will always know when I read this page what I was writing about- even when I'm 100 years old sipping tea in my summer kitchen.

"Wisdom is one of the few things that looks bigger the further away it is."
Terry Pratchett,

Chapter 19

A loud pounding on the door woke me from a lovely dream.

In the dream, I was sitting in a chaise lounge on a beautiful veranda eating ice cream and wearing my new dress. I assumed I was in Italy because the veranda overlooked rolling hills lined with those funny looking Italian trees. You know, the ones that look like tall, fat pipe cleaners. Anyway, Jared came through some pretty French doors onto my veranda with an atlas in hand. As he tried to hand the book to me, it dropped. Instead of making one loud slam, the atlas just kept pounding over and over.

"Olivia, we need to talk." More pounding. It was my dad.

"What time is it?" I moaned.

"It's seven o'clock."

I sat up and rubbed my eyes. "Come in."

The door swung open and there my dad stood in a light blue tinted tank top with a big Minnie Mouse on it. There were

126

little red hearts surrounding Minnie's head. The shirt was probably three sizes too small. The seams under his arms and around his neck were about to explode and his hairy belly was sticking out.

I laughed. "Funny, Dad. Did you show Mom yet?"

"You think I'm wearing you mother's shirt as a joke?" He questioned.

"I hope so." I smirked.

"I'm wearing this because I couldn't find any of my own t-shirts." His voice took on an angry tone. He pointed to my three piles. "There!" he said. "You see, there are all of my shirts! You have your own shirts. Don't we buy you shirts?"

I just stared at him. He was so over reacting.

"Well, don't we?"

"Yeah," I said, offended by his tone.

He rubbed his forehead. "Then why are you wearing mine?"

"Because they're comfortable."

He sighed heavily, and then started digging through my piles until he was certain he had every one of his t-shirts. "Here," he said, tossing me two of his shirts. "You can have those. Hands off the rest."

"Sorry, Dad." I paused, stupidly remembering the bug filled porch light from the night before. "Oh, Dad, someone really needs to clean out the porch light shade. It's full of bug carcasses."

He grunted something before he left, but I had no idea what. With the mood he was in, I probably didn't want to know.

I just shrugged it off and snuggled back into my covers and tried to resurrect my dream.

––––––––––

The kitchen was quiet. Light poured in through the large window above the kitchen table and illuminated the remains of a box of doughnuts. I picked up a very greasy apple fritter and shoved it into my mouth as I followed the sound of voices that had rolled in from outside.

The voices led me to the garden. Mom and Penelope were busily chatting and picking squash blossoms to stuff and fry for dinner.

Mom looked up. "Hey, sleepyhead."

"Is Dad still ticked about his shirts?"

Mom smiled. "He was over it as soon as he had them back in his possession."

"Good."

"It was too bad he found his shirts so quickly." Penelope said, and sniffed a squash blossom.

"Why?" I asked. My dad's a bear when he's mad."

"Well, the picture of him I took isn't very good."

"You took my dad's picture?"

"A devilish grin spread across her face. "Yeah, I snuck out of my room when he was pounding on your door, but I was only able to get one taken before he went into your room. It's a side shot. Oh, well."

"Can I have a copy?"

"Olivia, it's not nice to make fun of your father." My mom reprimanded.

"Oh, come on, Mom! Can you imagine Dad's face on Christmas morning opening a picture of himself in your Minnie Mouse tank? It would be so funny!"

She laughed in spite of herself. "Yeah, make us a copy."

Penelope grinned as she nodded.

"Hey, Olivia!"

I looked up. It was my dad. He was back in his own shirt and standing by the barn. I looked anxiously to my mom.

"I told you." She paused to wipe sweat from her already heated face, though it was only nine-thirty in the morning. "He isn't mad. Go on over. I think he's feeling bad about yelling at you earlier."

Dad was waving. "Come on and bring Penelope."

I looked to Penelope. She smiled. "Let's go."

"Okay, Dad. We're coming." I called back and trotted

towards the barn with Penelope close behind.

Beads of sweat had started to form on my face. Not because of the outside temperature as much as because a spark of fear had ignited inside of me. We were following my dad who had just disappeared to the back of the barn- where the tire swing was. The tire swing that I had cut with a pocketknife. The tire swing that was too weak now to hold much more than a small dog. I turned and smiled weakly at Penelope who was keeping time with my ever slowing pace.

"Something wrong?"

"No." I said, not bothering to give her an explanation for my lapse in speed.

"So, why are you walking so slow?" She was now beside me.

"I didn't know I was. I'm sorry."

Penelope shrugged then jogged past me. Pangs of panic bubbled and churned within me. My stomach started to ache and I couldn't breathe. I came to a stop and put my head between my legs. He wouldn't be taking us to the swing. No. No way.

I tried to think of a hundred other reasons he would he would have to take us behind the barn. Maybe he wanted us to feed the chickens. Of course! That had to be it- the chickens!

No need to panic, Olivia, I said to myself over and over. We are just going to feed the chickens. Yeah, that's it. And it would be a really great experience for Penelope too. Dad's smart. He would want her to embrace the country experience whole-heartedly. I stood back up and took a confident breath.

"The chickens." I said, and began my journey to the backside of the barn.

As I came around the corner, I noticed the tall grass that usually stayed green under the arms of the giant maple had started to dry- its shade too weak for the overbearing sun. Daisy, our duck, was still noisily waddling her usual circles and the chickens... Well... they weren't being fed.

My Dad and Penelope weren't anywhere near the chickens. They were standing next to my swing. My dad was animatedly telling Penelope the story of how he got the tire swing up and Penelope, in turn, giggled in all the right parts. As for me, I tried to think of a distraction as quickly as I could.

"Hey, Penelope," I called. "I'll bet you've never fed chickens before. Would you like to?"

"Would I like to do what?" She questioned.

"Feed the chickens." I said, motioning her back toward the coop.

"I already fed them." Dad said. "You girls can feed them tomorrow, though."

Penelope gave him an unenthusiastic, "cool."

"Olivia, come on over, I was just telling Penelope about all the fun we've had with this *old* tire swing." He emphasized old and gave the swing a push. It swayed gently under his pressure.

"We sure have had a lot of fun, Dad." I managed a weak laugh, as I walked over to where they stood. "Well, it's been really cool reminiscing, but me and Penelope are going over to Katie's, so we gotta run."

"We do?"

I narrowed my eyes. "Yeah. I must have forgotten to tell you." I tugged on her arm. "Come on."

"Can't Katie wait?" Dad sounded a little hurt. I thought we could show Penelope how a real swing works." He gave the swing a harder push. I watched as it reached up into the leafy canopy and half expected to come apart before dad caught it. But it didn't. He patted the tire. "Get in, Livvy."

"Dad, I don't feel so well."

He sighed heavily. I felt bad that I had hurt his feelings, but better that than my backside.

At about that time I caught that Penelope knew something was wrong. Not with me, but with the swing. She was looking directly at me, her face tightened and arms crossed.

"How bout it, Penny?" Dad wouldn't give it up. "Better than a carnival ride."

Penelope was absolutely glowering at me as she said,

solemnly, "I'm not feeling so good, either, Uncle Steve. Maybe another day."

I was feeling pretty stupid. Penelope was silently letting me know that she knew that I did, indeed, cut the rope. And Dad, well, he looked like his playground buddies had just abandoned him for the teeter-totters.

I didn't have the guts to say anything to him as Penelope and I started to walk away. But I did feel a small sense of relief, even though it had come at a cost. Guilt sucks. As with all of my ill attempts at deception, this plan too, went spinning out of control. Before we had taken three or four steps- we heard, "WEEEEE!"

I looked desperately to Penelope who was shaking her head in disgust. I caught sight of my father who was swinging the tire swing so high that I wasn't sure what to be more worried about, the swing flipping completely around the branch or the rope breaking.

"DAD, STOP!" I yelled and started toward him. But it was too late. With a loud SNAP of the rope, he came crashing to the ground.

"Dad! Are you all right?" I was beside him in seconds. He was quiet for a moment causing my heart to race. "Dad, please be okay."

I heard a moan and in a barely audible voice he said, "I'm okay."

Penelope was beside me now. "Uncle Steve, maybe you shouldn't try to move. Let me get Aunt Claire.

"No, no." He slowly sat up- uncoiling the tattered rope from around his body. "I'll be fine. I just need a moment. He shook his head and started to slowly move his hands, then arms and finally toes and legs. "Nothing broken." He said, slowly standing up. "Wow, I am so glad that it wasn't one of you girls in the swing. That would have been a disaster." He picked up the wasted end of rope. "You know, this shouldn't have happened. I would have sworn that this rope had a lot of years left on it." He shook his head.

"Are you sure that you're okay, Uncle Steve?"

"Yes, I'm really okay. Thanks, honey." He examined the broken end.

I felt like crap. I couldn't say or do anything. As far as dad was concerned the rope broke because of exposure and part of me was happy to keep it that way. I quickly calculated the reasons why it was best to keep him uninformed: I wouldn't be grounded for the rest of my life, I wouldn't be a disappointment, I would probably get a new swing, I wouldn't feel guilt.

But wait a minute; I did feel guilt and Penelope still scowling at me didn't help matters.

"You know," Dad said, and turned back towards us with the rope. If I didn't know better, I'd swear this rope was cut." He brought it close, so we could examine it.

"Oh, really," Penelope said, sarcastically. " I wonder why someone would do that?"

"Oh, Penelope, I don't really think anybody would have or could have for that matter." Dad scratched his head. "Maybe it was a defect in the…"

"I cut the rope." I said, before he could finish his sentence.

"What?"

I couldn't stand to look at him. "I cut the rope." I said it again just above a whisper this time.

"Livvy, why?" He stumbled over his words. "How?"

"I was trying to get back at Penelope for ruining my summer." I shot them both quick glances then turned my gaze back to the dry grass. It's pretty pathetic when hardened ground looks more sympathetic then my own family. I did it with my pocket knife." I couldn't bear to look at my dad. Seeing the furrowed brow, tightened lips and disappointed stare was more than I could take.

I heard him sigh heavily as he stood. He was muttering things under his breath that I probably shouldn't repeat. I kept my gaze low and waited for him to blow up. But he didn't. He just walked away. I felt horrible. I was lower than low; I was a maggot. I wanted to run after him and beg his forgiveness, but I didn't. Something told me it was best to keep out of his way. I had disappointed him. I was the last person he wanted to see right now.

"I suppose you hate me too," I said, not lifting my gaze.

Penelope didn't respond.

"Well, I'm outa here," I said. Penelope was ticked at me too and rightfully so. I needed to take a long walk.

I had gotten tot the end of our drive and was about to step onto the road when I heard Penelope's voice. "Hey," she said, trotting to catch up with me. "Where are you going?"

"I thought you were mad at me."

"I was." She smiled. "But, by the way your dad marched off, I figured you need an ally."

"I'm sorry." Cutting the rope was stupid. I could've hurt you."

"You didn't."

"But, I was trying."

"I know." She wrapped her arm around mine, and we walked together under an assertive sun.

"After all, what's a life, anyway? We're born, we live a little while, we die."
E.B. White

Chapter 20

We were quiet as we walked. My mind was preoccupied with the unavoidable lecture I would have to endure as soon as Dad cooled off. Of course, I would be grounded, that was just as unavoidable as the lecture, but being grounded was nothing compared to the lecture. Lectures stunk because I'm forced to stare at my parents as they proceed to tell me why I was wrong. I knew I was wrong. The guilt that was twisting my gut into a million knots told me so. I didn't need them to remind me.

We were coming upon the Wahl's house. Butterflies fluttered about my already twisted gut, as a flashback of Jared kissing my hand flooded my memory. I must have slowed my pace.

"Why are we stopping here?" Penelope smirked. "Are we stopping to visit *someone*?" She jabbed me with her elbow.

"I wasn't aware I had stopped." I felt flustered. "I guess I was daydreaming."

"I'll bet." She giggled. "Well?"

"Well, what? Let's keep walking."

"Come on." She tugged on my arm. "It's perfect. I know you want to see him."

"Oh, my gosh! I can't believe this." I pulled on Penelope's arm. "Let's go!"

"Come on!" She was pulling me towards the Wahl's drive and I was tugging her towards the road. I was starting to get a bit irritated when we heard the first scream. We both stopped.

"What was that?" Penelope asked, still grasping my arm.

"If I didn't know better," I answered, "I would say it was a banshee."

There was another sharper scream, followed by a low sorrowful moaning sound.

We both jumped. I grabbed my chest. Guilt and puppy love had already assaulted my digestive system. Believe me, throwing fear in, didn't do my body any favors. I felt like I was going to throw-up and have a heart attack at the same time.

"That's coming from the Wahl's garden." Penelope's voice was small.

"It sounds like someone's in trouble. Maybe we should help." I said, unconvincingly.

Another scream.

"Oh, my gosh!" I had come to a terrifying conclusion. "That's Diane Wahl!"

It had struck Penelope, too. She started running toward the garden. "The baby!" She cried, as she ran.

I took off after Penelope and did my best to stay on her heels until we arrived at the garden gate.

All was quiet when we got to the garden. The only sound I heard was the tired sighs of the cottonwood trees as an exasperated breeze tried to stir up the hot air. "Diane!" I hollered. No response, only the sound of my own voice echoing back to me off their ancient red barn. "Diane! It's me, Livvy!" Livvy-ivvy-ivvy, answered the ancient red barn.

"Maybe, we should split up and look for her."

Penelope suggested.

"I thought the sound was coming from this area," I said. "Maybe, we were just hearing things."

Before the pleasant possibility could take root, we heard Diane sobbing. "Livvy, help me." She sounded hollow. Helpless.

"The herb garden." I pointed.

We hurried into the section marked 'kitchen herbs.' We ran through parsley and thyme, jumped over shrubs or rosemary and mounds of tarragon, and skirted round the dill and fennel. We stopped when we reached the section marked 'sage.'

She was on her back. Her skirt was raised, and her legs open, exposing herself. If you looked closely, you could see the crown of the baby's head.

"It's okay." I said, as we raced to her side. The sage slapped our legs and crushed under our heavy steps, releasing it pungent fragrance.

She was drenched in sweat and desperately trying to keep control.

"What happened?" I asked, trying to hide the terror that was quickly building inside of me.

"I need someone to call 911." She looked to Penelope.

Penelope shook her head and made a scramble to the house.

"The baby," she said between contractions. "Decided it was time." She squeezed my hand and let free another low moan. "It's different. There's something wrong."

"I saw the baby's head." I tried my best to console her. "Maybe if you push really hard-"

Diane was shaking her head. "No, there's something wrong. Please, check again."

I crouched down between her legs. There was something rounded trying to push out, but it wasn't a head.

"There's an ambulance on the way." Penelope had returned out of breath. She crouched down beside me. Her face was masked with panic.

"I think it the baby's bottom coming." I said, my voice wavering.

Diane cried out again.

I suddenly felt like I was slipping- as if my inner self was being sucked into a vacuum. The scary thing was, I wanted to go there. I wanted to disappear. I wanted to somehow slip back in time. I pictured myself on my tire swing. My dad was pushing me and I was giggling as I outstretched my hand and tried to pluck the stars from the night sky.

I had never seen a normal birth before, let alone a breech birth. I was afraid. Angry questions bubbled in my mind. Where was the ambulance? Where was Victor? Where was Jared? Why me?

Another cry, and instantly I was back in the sage. I desperately tried to keep control. I looked to Penelope, who had moved and was now holding Diane's hand and whispering words of comfort.

Old Winder sniffed his way to the garden. He panted behind me and I could feel the heat of his breath on my back. "Go away!" I snapped. Go lay down!" He crept several yards back and made a bed in the dirt.

More cries. And I watched as the baby's bottom pushed out farther. Was there always this much blood when babies were born? I wanted to throw-up, but I was too scared. "The baby's starting to come out." I said. "I don't know what to do. Should I pull it out?"

"I don't know!" Penelope's voice was frantic.

That's when Winder started barking. "Hush boy," I said. But he wouldn't stop. Loud yelps punctuated by mournful howls saturated my brain. "Stop it, Winder!" There's no one there!" My voice was desperate and my hands trembled.

I didn't want Diane or her baby to die. Not here- not like this. But I was fast losing control and I didn't know what to do. The urge to run was bubbling inside of me.

At that time, something strange happened. I can't

really explain it. A female voice- clear and sweet spoke in my head. At first, I thought that I had finally gone over the edge. Hearing voices. Officially insane. But with every singsong syllable she whispered, I felt calmer and calmer.

"Hush, child," she whispered. "You must stay calm. Diane needs you now. No time for selfish thoughts."

I looked to Penelope to see if she heard anything. She was busy helping Diane keep focused. I didn't think she heard a thing.

I reached to pull out the baby. "Wait, child." The voice whispered. "Not yet. Stay calm and don't encourage Diane to push until she feels she needs to."

"You're doing good, Diane," I said. "The baby's coming out."

Diane was swathed in sweat- a sweat that was laced with tears and pain. Her eyes were blood shot. I wasn't sure she heard me. But before she cried out one again, we locked eyes and she shook her head.

The baby pushed out farther.

"You're doing so good!" I called out. And I could see the child, who had decided to come into this world in a twisted backwards way, was a girl. It became real. She had become real. Tears flooded my eyes. "Your baby girl needs you, Diane. You can do this."

Penelope smiled. "Did you hear," she spoke gently. "It's a girl."

Diane's mouth turned up and a spark flickered in her tired eyes.

More cries. The baby's legs unfolded and she was pushed to her navel. I could see the cord.

"Olivia," the voice said. "It's time. The baby needs to get out. You need to stay calm and on her next contraction encourage her to push hard. It's important.

Diane yelled out.

"Push hard, Diane! Please, the baby's almost out!"

She was squeezing Penelope's hand. "Push, Diane!" Penelope said. "Push!"

"Olivia," the voice whispered. "Pull gently, on the baby's legs."

I grasped the tiny legs and gently pulled. I was worried about pulling too hard. What if I pulled them off? It wasn't like a doll. Mama wouldn't be able to put her back together.

But before my mind had too much, with a whoosh of bloody liquid, the baby was out. I tried the best I could to support the slippery little bundle, which was still attached by her cord.

"Diane!" Penelope cried out. "Diane!"

I looked up. Diane lay still.

"Livvy, she won't wake up." Penelope listened at her chest. "I still hear a heartbeat." Her face was flushed and her eyes glazed with tears.

"The baby's not breathing." The words seem to catch in my throat. I looked at the lifeless child in my hands

Penelope came to my side. "What's wrong with her?"

"I think she's dead."

"She can't be."

Winder started to bark again. "Shut up, you stupid dog!" I sobbed "Shut up!"

"Now, girls," a voice came from behind us in the same sweet tones of the voice that whispered in my mind. "Don't cry."

This time we both heard it. We turned. It was Ms. Stella. I hadn't been this happy to see another person in my entire life.

"The baby's not breathing." I managed to say between sobs.

She bent over us. "Wrap her in a cloth," she said, pointing to the white cloth that had spilled from Diane's gathering basket. Penelope picked up the cloth and we awkwardly wrapped the baby.

"Now then, give her a few seconds, she'll come around." She paused. "They're okay girls," Ms. Stella reassured us. "They're both going to be fine."

As the wail from the ambulance filled the air, the tiny

baby girl took a breath. Her vibrating cries were music to our ears. We smiled at each other- then looked to Ms. Stella.

She was smiling too. "You did good, girls," she said. "You both did real good."

"What happened?" Jared's voice was filled with panic. He was running towards us with the twins close behind.

"Don't bring the twins any farther." Penelope stood, blocking the scene. "You're mom and you're little sister are going to be fine."

Tears swelled in Jared's eyes. He squatted, holding his brothers close to him. "I shouldn't have left her. She was feeling weird and wanted me to take the boys for a walk." He shook his head. I should have stayed."

'Is our baby born?" Caleb asked.

Jared shook his head. The siren stopped as the ambulance pulled into the drive. "Why don't we go and get the nice people and show them where Mommy and the baby are?"

"Okay." Elijah said, taking off in front of his brothers.

Pure joy filled my heart as I heard the first coos of the little girl. "Thank you, Ms. Stella for..." I looked around.

"Where'd she go?" Penelope seemed as confused as I was.

"I don't know."

A rush of organized confusion flooded the garden. We were shuffled back as the part-time EMTs took over. I knew them all and watched intently as Mr. Seymour from the grocery store, and Ms. Peggy, the librarian, pulled out the stretcher.

"Why don't you go on home now, Olivia," the man I knew as the school janitor, said. "We've got everything under control."

I motioned for Penelope, who was crouched beneath a tree. Visibly shaken, she got up slowly. We left the scene unnoticed- unsung.

"How could such sweet and wholesome hours
Be reckoned but with herbs and flowers?"
Andrew Marvel

Chapter 21

Dad was waiting for me on the porch. His arms were crossed and he was wearing just a hint of a scowl. His expression vanished when he saw us walk up the drive-covered with blood- our faces strained.

"Oh, my God!" He said. "What happened?"

I melted into my Dad's arms. "Daddy," I said. "I was so scared." I started sobbing uncontrollably. Penelope was crying too. Dad held us both.

"You're home now," he said. "Everything's okay."

Mom had heard the commotion. "What happened?" She said, coming up the front steps.

Sobbing, I went to her. She rocked me in her arms until the sting of what we had experienced numbed.

After we calmed down, we told Mom and Dad what had happened.

"I'm so proud of you both," Mom said, and placed the phone back in the receiver. "Victor says, Diane and the baby are doing fine. They're both asleep."

"No telling what would have happened if you two hadn't shown up." Dad shook his head.

"I'm just glad Ms. Stella showed up when *she* did. If she hadn't been there to guide us, I would have completely freaked out." I shuddered at the thought.

"I wonder why she didn't stick around?" Penelope asked.

I shrugged. "I don't know. I'm still trying to figure out how she was whispering instructions in my ear."

"Yeah, because I didn't see her until after the baby was born." Penelope said.

Mom gathered us both in her arms, "I'm just *so* proud." She said, squeezing us. "Now, why don't you both get cleaned up? You'll certainly feel better after a shower."

"Go ahead and take a shower first," I said to Penelope.

She smiled. "Are you sure?"

I pushed her. Hurry. This blood is creeping me out." I held up my hands- the dried flaky blood seemed so surreal. I could smell it. I could taste it- metallic on the back of my throat.

My mind drifted back- the sage- the cries- the confusion- Ms. Stella. It felt as though it had happened a hundred years before. Just a dream. But the blood was there, cracking and flaking with every bend of my hand. The blood reminded me it was real.

"I'll have to be sure to thank Ms. Stella for helping you." Mom patted the top of my head. "What kind of pie should I make for her this time?" She giggled. I suppose she found herself humorous.

I didn't react. Though I heard her—I was still in the sage.

It felt good to be clean and cozy under crisp cotton sheets. I pulled out my moon journal- flipping through the thick pages. I stopped at the page laced with sage leaves. The fragrance took me back to the events that had occurred earlier. I took my pen in hand and wrote:

Today, me and Penelope helped deliver a baby. Mom told me I'm blessed to have been part of such a glorious event. She said Diane was lucky we were there. I'm not convinced. She told me that one day, after my anxiety has passed, I'd be glad I was there to help. She said we were wise beyond our years.

I don't think she understands how scared I was. If it wasn't for Ms. Stella, I think I may have bolted. I don't feel very brave (let alone wise). A truly brave person would have never have had that instinct.

Lovely scents stirred my senses and I awoke to a bedroom full of flowers. Bouquets had arrived early that morning from people all over town. The word was out. Penelope and I were officially deemed as heroes.

The most flamboyant bouquet was from the Wahls. Three-dozen bright red, long stemmed roses with lacy clusters of Queen Anne's lace and eucalyptus tucked amongst them. The card simply read, 'Our Hero.' Other bouquets also decorated my room: daises from the ambulance crew, carnations from the library, a mug filled with baby roses and bay's breath from the Harrisons, Peonies from Orchard Mill Bed and Breakfast.

Penelope burst through my door. She was beaming. "I have the same flowers," she said. "It's the coolest thing. I wonder if the newspaper will interview us?"

"Our town doesn't have a newspaper." I chuckled. "We have a *newsletter*."

"Oh." She seemed disappointed.

"I'm sure they'll write something nice." I wanted to make her feel better.

The morning was a flurry of incoming calls. Just about everybody in town called, except for the Frostmans and the Johnsons (We didn't care to hear from them anyway). Dad had gone to chop wood with old Man Massingale, so Mom took care of the calls. She beamed, as she retold the story, over and over.

When Katie called I decided to take it.

"So," she said. "How does it feel to be a hero?"

"The same as it feels to be a loser." I sighed. "So, what have you been up to?"

She ignored my attempt to change the subject. "I don't understand how you guys did it. Man, I would have been a mess."

"Believe me, I was a mess. I was about to take off running, but Ms. Stella showed up." I though a moment, "I wonder if she's getting as much attention as us? She's the real hero in this story."

The line was quiet. "Hello, Katie- you still with me? Hello."

"Livvy," she finally answered. "How could Ms. Stella have helped you?"

"By talking us through it." I chuckled. "How do you think?"

"I just think that's a little weird since she was found dead yesterday."

This time it was me who was quiet. "Oh, give me a break, Katie." I finally sputtered. "Who told you that?" You know, you can't believe *everything* you hear."

"Olivia," she said quietly. "My dad found her. He had gone there yesterday morning to remove a rotting tree. She had died in her sleep sometime the night before."

My mind began to spin. I felt like I was on an out of control carnival ride and I desperately wanted off. I dropped the phone and ran to the front porch, where I collapsed in a pool of tears.

"Olivia," my mom called out. She and Penelope ran after me. "Livvy, honey," she said, clutching me. "What's wrong?"

"Katie just told me Ms. Stella was found dead."

Penelope gasped.

"Oh, baby," Mom comforted me. "She was old. These things happen." She became wistful. "She was a wonderful, eccentric woman. I'm really going to miss her."

"You don't understand. She was found dead *yesterday* morning."

Penelope sat beside me. "Katie must have the story mixed up," she said, patting my hand. "We saw Ms. Stella yesterday. She helped us."

"It was her dad who found her. He went to Ms. Stella's cottage to do some work and she was dead." I sniffed. "They say she died the night before."

Mom stood. "I'm going to do a little research. This doesn't

make any kind of sense." She strode purposely into the house.

We sat on the porch for quite some time waiting for mom to come back out. The breeze picked up (right on time) and tickled the wind chimes. The screen door finally whined and Mom stood quiet-as if to gather her thoughts.

"Okay," She finally said, as she sat down between us. "Are you both completely sure that it was Ms. Stella who had helped you at Diane's?"

We both nodded.

She sighed. "It took a couple of calls, but yes, she was found dead on arrival yesterday morning. She had died in her sleep the night before."

Penelope's eyes narrowed. "I don't understand. She was there Aunt Claire. We both saw her."

"You believe us don't you?" I asked.

Mom was quiet. She put an arm around each of us before she spoke. "Sometimes, I believe people are put in our lives to teach us something. And I also believe that even after their death, that maybe, they stick around- just to make sure we're doing okay."

I sniffed. "You mean, like a guardian angel?"

"Yeah." She smiled.

I though about it for a while, and then smiled. Somehow, I was strangely comforted by the idea. In a way, it made sense.

The rest of the day slipped by lazily- like a slow running stream. The day whispered.

I thought back over what had happened in the sage and I no longer thought of myself as a coward. I felt privileged. Privileged to have experienced what we did and to have gained something from it… Wisdom.

"Knowing yourself is the beginning of all wisdom."
Aristotle

Chapter 22

Dad had come home just in time for dinner. When he saw it was frozen pizza, his face dropped. He grabbed a couple slices and was back out the door.

A couple hours later, he returned. It was 9:30pm. The sky was deep dusky gray and the evening star sparkled against it- a diamond on gray felt.

"Girls, I have something to show you. Come on outside." He motioned for us to follow.

We stumbled behind in the half-light of the summer's night. We passed through the garden and back around the barn, where the chickens were roosting and Daisy Duck snoozed softly in a mound of hay.

"My tire swing!" I exclaimed.

There it was, swaying softly back and forth in a breeze that seemed to stir from nowhere.

Dad smiled proudly. "I spliced the ends back together," he said, giving the rope a sturdy tug.

"Will it hold?" Penelope asked.

"Stronger than before." He winked. "Get on."

146

We both crawled into the tire- giggling and squirming.

He pulled back, and then with an extraordinary amount of power, pushed us toward the night sky. The sky was deepening- and the stars twinkled as they rose from the sweeping indigo blanket.

To the east, above the black cragged peaks of the Cascades, I saw the constellation Cygnus, the swan. I imagined I was on the swan's back flying over trees and mountains, clean up to heaven.

Ms. Stella was there, smiling at me. She winked and gave me a nod of approval.

I winked back.

Then, suddenly, I was back in the swing, giggling with my cousin. My friend. "Do this." I said, extending a hand as high as I could reach.

"Why?" Penelope asked, but did the same anyway.

"So we can pluck the stars from the sky." I said.

We both laughed as we reached for the stars. A low rumbling noise rose from behind the mountains.

"Do you hear that?" Dad said. "Sounds like thunder." "Thunder means rain!" I exclaimed.

Dad pulled our swing to a stop and we gathered under the giant arms of the maple and waited for more.

Mom, too, joined us as rumble after rumble rose from behind the shadowy mountains. "I've never been so excited to see rain in my entire life." She commented and put an arm around Dad's waist.

Soon, a black mass began to boil over the Cascade's sharp peaks. The wind rode on waves- carrying with it the sweet fragrance of the approaching storm. The long grass in the surrounding fields rustled and the leaves trembled. And if you listened closely enough, you could hear them say- *it's coming. The rain is coming.*

We cheered as the first big plops hit the earth. Then suddenly, the heavens unzipped, pouring its contents upon the dry land. We danced and laughed in the warm sweet rain. The thunder boomed overhead and we squealed with each bellow. Even my parents were laughing and dancing in the rain.

As the storm rolled past, we walked, drenched, back to the house. An eerie glow followed the storm, and with it, headlights pulled into our drive. It was a black Mercedes.

We stood, like a family of drowned rats, as Uncle Tom hopped out of the driver's seat.

"Daddy?" Penelope's voice was small.

"Penelope!" he hollered, arms spread wide.

Penelope's wet clothes squeaked as she ran with open arms to her father's open arms. The passenger's side door opened, revealing a long sleek set of dark legs. Aunt Desta slid out, looking like a goddess, as she stood. "Did you miss us?" She said, waiting for her wet hug.

I looked to my parents. "I thought she was supposed to be here two more weeks."

"You know my brother," Dad said. "Extremely unpredictable." He straightened up, plastered a conspicuously fake smile on his face and went to welcome his brother.

Mom tried to adjust her hair. "Desta, you're early," she said. "I hope there wasn't a problem."

"Not really," Aunt Desta answered. "A little unexpected business." She paused. "I tried to call earlier, but I couldn't get through."

As they made trivial small talk, I sunk back into that very corner of my mind where I felt safe. Their voices moved around me like strange music. Their movements became slow- an ancient form of social dance. I was lost in thought. Summer memories played before me like an old forgotten movie. I couldn't believe it was ending.

Penelope was happy to see her parents. She would be going back to the city tonight. Back to her large plush bedroom, back to her ballet lesson, back to shopping at her favorite boutiques, back to strolling through the marketplace, museums and galleries.

I would go back to my old life too. Riding horses, sleepovers with Katie, climbing trees and swimming in the slough, would become commonplace again. But what of us? Would we become estranged? Forget what we had learned? Hate each other for stupid reasons all over again?

Not if I had anything to do with it.

As our parents busily loaded luggage and souvenirs, Penelope and I said our goodbyes.

"Time flies when you're having fun." I said, wishing I had

been cleverer.

"Yeah," she said. "I can't believe they came back so early."

"You missed them?"

She thought for a moment. "Yeah," she said. "I did."

"Well," I said, trying not to cry. "I'm sure going to miss you. I liked having a sister for a while."

Tears streamed down her cheek. "So did I."

We hugged each other for a long time.

"Penelope, honey," Aunt Desta called. "It's time to go."

"Okay, Mom," Penelope answered. "I'll be right there." Penelope dug a folded up piece of paper out of her small handbag. "Here," she said, handing it to me. "It's my personal cell phone number. "We can talk for as long as we want. I have unlimited minutes.

"I promise I'll call often." I grabbed her hands. Tears flooded my eyes.

"Penelope, we have a long drive." Uncle Tom prodded.

Penelope wiped her eyes. "Thank you for everything," she said, and crawled into the back of the shiny black Mercedes. The doors closed and they sped off.

I stood in the quiet of the night. I was there long after the last flash of red from their taillights passed round the corner. I had already missed her.

When I finally decided it was time I go to bed, the first traces of morning had already streaked the sky red. Birds had begun twittering and our pathetic old rooster was attempting to crow.

I pulled out my moon journal and flipped through its aromatic pages. I read what I had written about Jared and laughed at the memory. Then I remembered something I had written but never finished. I flipped back to the page marked with roses.

The last line read:

The most important love of all...well...

I smiled and put pen to paper.

The most important love of all...well... to love one's self. How can you accept others if you can't even accept who you are?

A sage taught me that.

Summer Sage

Epilogue

September finally rolled around- bringing with it filtered yellow light. Shadows stretched as long as the yard. The dew glistened on the pumpkins long into the afternoon and the smell of ripe apples perfumed the air.

September also brought Diane Wahl back into her garden. She made me and Penelope Godmothers to baby Stella, a beautiful redheaded cherub, who Diane brings over often.

One amber tinted afternoon, Jared and I walked to Fern Cottage. I hadn't been there since Ms. Stella's death. It felt weird. Flowerbeds lay overgrown and the summer kitchen had been taken over by a family of raccoons.

I saw the basket she used for gathering her treasures and I decided to take it with me. I didn't think she would have minded. I now use it to store my treasures.

September also means school. Penelope (always the fashion queen) sent an outfit she thought would be perfect for me to wear on my first day of Junior High. It was a plaid skirt and brown turtleneck and penny loafers.

As I entered through the large double doors, the smell of fresh varnish and chewing gum dominated the halls. I wasn't at all nervous about being there because our Junior High and Elementary Schools are in the same building, so basically, I saw all the same kids. The only faces that were new were the kindergartners, and I knew most of them too.

I came in feeling very feminine in my chic new outfit, my hair was upswept (Mom helped) and I was wearing just a hint of makeup. My peers didn't take much notice (they never do), but Ms. Gilmore, my 6th grade teacher stopped in her tracks.

"Olivia?" She clasped her hands together. "This can't be the same child who left here last summer in those horrible ripped shorts and all that hair hanging in her face."

I smiled. "It's me, all right."

"I'm so pleased." She seemed to be in total awe. Then she looked down at my feet.

"Olivia!" Ms. Gilmore sighed, heavily. "Well, I guess it's a start." She shook her head as she teetered away on high heels.

I clicked the toes of my cowboy boots together. They were scuffed and worn, but hey, I was wearing socks and they were comfortable. You really didn't think I'd be caught in penny loafers did you?

Made in the USA
San Bernardino, CA
25 March 2018